Summer's Edge

"What do you want from me, Alice?"

The answer was so easy. She reached up around his neck and his arms went around her and his lips were on hers. Their mouths opened, his tongue intertwined with hers. It was sweet, sensuous.

She smelled his scent, she had grown to crave it. His skin, the faint soap or aftershave he used, the cotton of his shirt.

Her hands felt the nape of his neck, the shape of it, how it tapered to his collar. His hair was cropped so short she could feel the gradient from hair to skin.

"You," she said as he buried his face in her neck and her hair, breathing her in as well. "I want you."

"God, Alice…" she loved how he said her name, his accent, the rasp in his voice that betrayed his desire for her. His need. He's fighting it, she thought, but he needs this as much as I do.

Forbidden Lessons

"This is something that could ruin both our lives."

When 18-year-old Laura first sees her new German teacher her world is turned upside down. She can't get Mr Rydell out of her mind. Is it coincidence that she keeps bumping into him outside class or does he share her feelings? He's totally forbidden fruit. But the two of them are soon risking everything for passion.

Every rule is broken… who will be forced to pay the price?

Set in the UK in the 1980s, "Forbidden Lessons" is based on a true story.

Available in paperback or eBook from Lulu.com

SUMMER'S EDGE

by

Noël Cades

First Printing, 2014

ISBN: 0992501725
ISBN-13: 978-0-9925017-2-3

To Caroline

PART I

Opening

For now the wine made summer in his veins,
Let his eye rove in following

Idylls of the King: The Marriage of Geraint
Alfred, Lord Tennyson

1. Start of the end

All work and no play. That was the vow for this school term, their final term ever. Parties were banned. No boys. No fun. Nothing but study and revision until exams were over.

It was the plan anyway. Once they were through it they could enjoy the summer and endless freedom.

"I hope we don't end up dull girls," Alice said. She was walking to the first assembly of term with her two best friends. Strange to think that this routine of lining up and shuffling into their various rows would soon be over. It had been a morning ritual for years.

"Never." Jules had always been the wildest and most rebellious of them and was having to make the biggest effort to knuckle down this term. "I'll be partying for at least a year afterwards."

It was late April and the world still smelt like spring rather than early summer. The last of the daffodils were still out. They matched Fairmount's school colours of bottle green and gold and were planted everywhere.

Alice laughed. She felt in sudden high spirits, despite the huge, overwhelming cloud of A-levels that hung on the horizon. At least the first exams were still a month away. Right now the sun was shining, the sky was cool and blue and clear, and even if they had to suffer the Headmaster droning on for the next hour it was going to be a perfect day.

Becky was the most nervous about exams. "I just can't wait for them all to be over. I get this horrible feeling in my stomach just thinking about them, getting closer every day."

In Alice's mind the two-month wait afterwards to get their results would be more of an ordeal. But she didn't want to stress Becky out any more by mentioning it. She tried to reassure Becky but she felt the same flicker of panic herself from time to time. So many of their future plans rested on their A-levels.

Inside the hall there was the usual sense of restlessness at the start of term. Rustling and fidgeting and hushed whispers. Many people were still catching up with friends they hadn't seen over the holidays and being herded into the assembly hall limited chatter.

Alice, Jules and Becky sat together in the same row on the grey plastic interlocking chairs that had to be stacked and unstacked every day. It was a chore they wouldn't miss.

For the first assembly of term the teaching staff sat on the stage behind Mr Francis, the Headmaster, rather than at the back of the hall. It was always more relaxed - and easier for surreptitious conversation - not having teachers' eyes on the back of your head.

Alice was still searching for other friends of hers in the crowd when Jules gave her a sharp nudge.

"Who's that guy?" Jules indicated the stage.

She saw instantly whom Jules was referring to. Sitting beside the regular staff, who looked just the same as they always did, was an unknown man. He was tall and bronzed and exceptionally good looking.

Alice felt a jolt in her stomach. She wasn't the type for teacher crushes, but he was something else.

"Have any of the other teachers left?" she asked, wondering whom he might be a replacement for. She scanned the stage but all the staff that she could think of seemed to be there.

"Perhaps he's the new dinner lady," Jules said. Alice had to smother a laugh.

"He must be the new cricket coach," Becky whispered. Fairmount employed a dedicated coach for boys' cricket every summer term, usually a former professional player.

"He does look like a sportsman," Jules agreed.

Around them some other sixth form girls were also eyeing the new member of staff amid giggles and murmurs. Alice wondered if he realised how many curious eyes were upon him.

The buzz of conversation continued until everyone was inside and seated and the order was given for silence.

Sure enough, Mr Francis eventually informed them that Mr Walker, who was from Australia, would be coaching the boys for cricket that term. "We look forward to a successful season and I am sure you will all make him very welcome."

"What a waste. Why can't they us get a tennis coach like that?" some girl said behind them.

"Or they should let us play cricket. It's so sexist," her neighbour replied.

Alice privately agreed. It was stupid being segregated for sport, with boys never getting a chance to play tennis either. After all men played at Wimbledon didn't they? Given the school's dismal prowess in cricket the previous year there might be more glory to be won by handing out a few racquets.

Various other announcements were made and the assembly closed, with Mr Francis and the staff leaving first. Many eyes were on the new coach as he walked out, tall and powerfully built and somehow out of place. Was it because he was new or because he was Australian? Alice wasn't sure.

Outside she was distracted from her thoughts by catching up with more old friends on the way to her first class, which was Chemistry.

She loved the chemistry lab with its stained and scarred benches, wooden racks of test tubes and Bunsen burners. There wouldn't be much time for practical experiments this term though, it was mainly theory.

Alice chose a seat on the back row by the window, being one of the first to arrive. Others filed in and then she saw a girl called Sarah Norris looking for somewhere to sit. Alice had always felt sorry for her as she was rather plain and unpopular. There was nothing wrong with her, she just ranked at the bottom of the social ladder by whatever arcane and unspoken method decided it.

Sarah tried to take a place near the front but one of the boys blocked her. "That's saved. Find somewhere else." She looked mortified.

We're too old for this, Alice thought. It was the last term, they would soon all be going their separate ways. It was time to do away with the meanness and the cliques. "Over here!" She waved Sarah into the seat next to her which she took gratefully.

A boy on the front row smirked and made a snide remark to his friend, deliberately audible. Alice ignored them. She was getting fed up with schoolboys; it was one of the reasons it had been easy to agree to their exam-term vow of no boys. At least when they started university the majority of guys would be older.

* * *

"Thank god our days of this are numbered. We should start a countdown to no-more-slop," said Jules as they stood in the queue for lunch.

The smell of school dinners permeated every brick and fibre of the dining hall. Plastic trays, stainless steel serving dishes, the slow shuffle along the line from cabbage to apple crumble. It was definitely one of the many things they wouldn't miss.

As sixth formers they were first in the queue and got to sit at the tables on the far side by the windows, unsupervised by teachers. It made it much easier to gossip but most people tried to get lunch over with as quickly as possible. The real socialising took place afterwards when people sat out on the lawns until the bell went for afternoon lessons.

Their resolution this term, of course, was to cut out all socialising and do nothing except study. But the sun was shining and the grass was newly mown and Alice couldn't face sitting in the dark and musty study room. Sunlight was probably good for the brain anyway.

"It's only the first day back, let's take our Economics notes outside," she suggested. "We can go straight from there to class."

The others needed no persuasion. Becky, who didn't do Economics, took some other work with her.

Of course they did no work. Lying back in the spring sunshine, the hope of getting a sun-tan by two o'clock took precedence.

Some other people they knew sat nearby and everyone discussed the dread of exams for a while. The start of term was traditionally a time for flirting and new relationships, but not this term. Everyone was in a more serious mood.

"We just have to get through this, then it's a year of freedom," Jules said.

Depending on their A-level results she and Alice planned to defer their university places and go backpacking for a year in South East Asia and Australia. If they didn't get the grades they needed they'd have to repeat their exams the next year at the sixth form college or choose different careers. So it was a big incentive to work hard this year.

A discussion began about gap years and different people's plans. There were others planning to backpack around Australia or South America, build schools in Africa, work at orphanages in India.

"Did you get your flights yet?" someone asked.

"No, we're going to wait for last minute bargains," Alice said. She wanted her travel budget to stretch as far as possible. If that meant flying on a dodgy airline taking half a dozen hops to get across Asia, so be it. Plus there was no point buying tickets now and then having to get a refund if she flunked out in August.

Still it was great to have something to focus on. She had an image of a beach in Thailand in her mind, of white sand and palm trees. It kept her going through the rainy days and revision. A whole year of summer: she was excited. It was so close.

2. The Dog & Duck

Fake student ID cost five quid and a passport photo, and you got it from some guy called Ricardo at the local sixth form college. Back in those days, you could still smile in your passport photo.

"We should get into the Dog & Duck before closing," Jules said. "There's going to be a lock in."

Their good resolutions had lasted less than a week. By Friday they had decided they needed to relax and let off some steam. Staying home and studying could wait for another week.

Turning eighteen should have meant they no longer needed the fake student cards. But so many bars seemed to have over 21 nights these days. The cards did their trick and the doorman waved them through.

Such a throng of people. That was the problem with popular places, they were always packed. You could never get to the bar, never get a table.

Alice started looking around for people they knew. She recognised some people she didn't know but whom they often saw in the same venues. She also saw some people she half knew. People you could nod and say hi to, but not strike up a conversation with.

There was no one else from their school anyway. Alice tried to elbow her way to the bar to order drinks.

"Oh my god!" Becky was shrieking. "That guy over there, it's the new cricket coach."

"From school? Are you sure?"

"Yes, it's definitely him." Alice looked over to where Becky was pointing, and saw him from the side. Outside of the school setting he seemed even more handsome.

"Does that mean other teachers are here?" Jules looked around. She didn't want to be caught out on the town with fake ID.

"No, he's with a group of guys. I don't recognise any of them."

Jules studied them. "I think some of them are county cricketers. That red-haired guy looks familiar, I think he's a bowler." Her father was into cricket and sometimes dragged her to matches. "We should go and introduce ourselves." Jules was always the bold one.

"We can't do that! What would he think, seeing us in here? He might report us," Becky was the least adventurous of the three.

"I doubt he'd recognise us. It's only a week since term started and it's not like any of us play cricket," Jules said.

"If he doesn't know who we are, we can hardly introduce ourselves then."

But Jules was already pushing through the crowd towards the group. The cricketers had also scored one of the few booth tables which increased their appeal. At the Dog & Duck a booth was the next best thing to a VIP lounge.

Alice had seen the new coach around school a few times over the past week and had developed a bit of a crush on him. She was far from the only one who found him attractive. Coming from Australia he was tanned and healthy looking while everyone else was still winter-pale. She saw Jules had worked her charm with the red-headed guy and was now waving them over to join her. Alice fought her way through following Becky, trying not to spill the three drinks she was carrying.

A bald man stepped back and bumped into her nearly sending her flying, and then turned round to give her an angry glare because some drink had splashed on him. It's your fault, Alice wanted to say, but didn't dare. Any hint of a fight and they'd all be thrown out.

A couple of the guys stood up so the girls could sit round the table and Alice found herself seated next to the school cricket coach. There was one other man about his age, early thirties she guessed, sitting on the other side of him. The rest of the group looked younger. She noticed Becky was already making eyes at one of them.

"I'm Stewart, and this is Chris." He introduced himself. So he obviously didn't recognise them. Alice knew of him as Mr Walker. Chris turned out to be an Australian as well, who was currently coaching the local county team.

"My dad's a huge cricket fan, he's hoping you'll do better this season," Jules told him. Gloucestershire had ended up close to the bottom of the table the previous year.

Chris grinned. "We'll do our best. These boys are some of the weapons we've brought over." He indicated a couple of the younger guys, including the one Becky liked. "Brett, Grant, true blue Aussie firepower."

"I thought you could only have one overseas player," Jules said.

"Grant has an English granny so he's impersonating one of us," the red-haired guy told her.

As the cricket talk continued Alice was enjoying the thrill of being pushed up against Mr Walker since as many people as possible were crammed in around the table. She was on the edge but if she moved away from him she would be falling off the bench. His hard, muscular thigh was pressed against hers and she could feel its warmth.

"Not much space in these English pubs is there?" he said to her.

She tried to apologise and move away but he laughed and stopped her by putting a hand on her thigh. It was a gesture to steady her, not a pass, but the heat of his hand even through her jeans made her shiver. He was so attractive. He had dark blonde hair, closely cropped, and grey blue eyes.

"So you're involved in cricket too?" she asked, knowing the answer full well.

"I'm coaching at a school near here. Chris set me up with the job." Alice felt a slight twinge of guilt since she also knew the school in question. He explained that he'd been injured last season and was still considering permanent retirement. "We'll see what the medics say. But I'm getting a bit old for this."

"How old are you?" she felt brave enough to ask.

He smiled, looking her straight in the eye. "Too old to be this close up against a young thing like you." She realised he was flirting with her. The attraction was mutual.

He didn't even know the half of it when it came to her age. He probably assumed she was at least twenty-one, not eighteen. But Alice wasn't going to let it deter her.

"I'm not that young," she lied. He laughed.

"It's a good thing I haven't drunk enough to lose all my self-control."

"You'd better have some more then." She looked him directly in the eye. She was shocked at herself for being so forward, but something carried her away.

At that moment one of the younger cricketers put a new round of drinks on the table.

Stewart Walker looked at Alice and took a beer. "You really want me to get hammered?"

"Down it in one," she challenged him. She wanted him to lose his inhibitions just a little bit more. She had no idea where she was going with this, she knew she was playing with fire but there was this electricity between them. She couldn't take her eyes off his lips. She wanted to feel them on hers, on her neck.

She wasn't sure how much anyone had drunk but she knew she'd had too many to have her wits fully about her. But she felt a lovely warm haziness sitting by him, by this guy who made her entire body tingle just by his proximity. He smelt amazing, an intoxicating male scent of clean sweat, soap and beer.

Suddenly Jules was tugging her arm. "I need to visit the ladies. Come with me."

Alice was reluctant, she was very happy where she was.

But Jules was fierce. "Come on."

The ladies loo was usually pretty awful by this time of night, water splashed everywhere with all the sinks clogged with wet tissues. Cigarette butts all over the floor. At least one cubicle was always out of order or had someone slumped and vomiting from drink. There were other girls queueing who gave them evil eyes.

"Do you actually need to go? The queue's forever." Alice said.

"I need to talk some sense into you. What the hell are you doing? You're practically falling all over him."

"It's not just me. He's been flirting back as well."

"That doesn't make it any better. For god's sake, Alice, how much have you drunk?"

"Becky's just as happy with that guy she's hanging off."

"He's not her teacher." Jules was worried.

"He's not really my teacher, is he? It's not like any of us play cricket. He's only here for a term anyway."

"I don't think he'll see it that way."

Alice looked at herself in the mirror. No matter how great you felt or how unsmudged your make up was, everyone looked like hell in the mirrors of the Dog & Duck. "I swear the lighting in here is designed to make people drink themselves to oblivion." She tried pinching her cheeks to look less pale. Her eyeliner was still in place and her hair was having a good night. How old did she look, she wondered? Twenty-one at least surely.

"Stop preening in front of the mirror and try to sober up."

"I'm honestly not that drunk. He's just so sexy, it's overpowering." Alice had drunk too much, but she knew she would still want to flirt with him even if she was sober.

"He's way too old for you," Jules said.

"He said that too."

"I should listen to him then, if I were you."

Returning to the table Alice made sure she was ahead of Jules so she could get her seat back. She wouldn't have put it past Jules to have taken her place to stop her sitting by Mr Walker. Jules was in such an annoying and uncharacteristically sensible mood.

"You're back," he said. A light came into his eyes even though he was clearly more drunk than before. He was glad she was back, Alice realised. It was enough to quash any more sensible intentions that Jules might have inspired in her.

"I'm back," she said and smiled at him. His eyes narrowed but his gaze didn't leave her.

She couldn't remember afterwards how long they sat there or how much more they drank or even if they held a coherent conversation. Alice was far from sober but she was more intoxicated by him than alcohol.

Jules had clearly given up on her and was talking with the red-haired guy and another couple of guys, probably more of the cricket team.

Then they were sitting there and he was looking at her and suddenly he was leaning towards her and his lips brushed hers. Only briefly, but they were warm and firm and a jolt ran from her lips to the pit of her stomach.

"You taste better than beer," he said in her ear.

"You didn't really get a proper taste," she said.

"This isn't wise."

"Does it matter?" she asked.

"It probably should."

And then his mouth was on hers again, and she felt his tongue entering her, exploring her as the kiss deepened. He probed her own mouth, wet and warm and intimate and making her want more of him, want him closer.

He wasn't even touching her elsewhere, they were solely kissing. But any contact with him was like electricity.

Some small part of her brain was freaking out: you're kissing Mr Walker! What the hell are you doing? but the rest of her was in ecstasy. She was reciprocating, wanting to taste him back, to drink him in.

There were cheers and catcalls when the other guys noticed.

"Oi Stewie, stop molesting that poor girl," one of them joked.

Alice opened her eyes to see Jules glaring at her with an accusatory expression. Becky was so drunk she barely noticed what Alice was up to. She was smiling foolishly, half draped over the cricketer she liked who appeared to be equally attracted.

Mr Walker broke off. "I don't think she needs rescuing. Do you?" he asked Alice.

She didn't answer but smiled at him and went to kiss him again to an even louder chorus.

"Alright lay it off, it's not a sideshow," Chris told the other guys. He was more in control of himself than the others, keeping an eye on his players. "None of you are going to be in any fit state tomorrow to play Somerset."

It was closing time anyway. Or rather chucking out time, since they were in a lock in and the landlord had finally had enough.

"Here's where I should ask for your number," he said.

Alice panicked slightly. She couldn't imagine how her mother would react if she picked up the phone to a strange Australian man, clearly not a schoolboy, asking for Alice. She also didn't want him to know that she still lived at home.

She noticed Becky writing her phone number down on a beermat for the guy she had been flirting with. If Mr Walker was really inclined to call her, he could reach her through Becky.

"Here's where I'm sure you'll figure out a way to find it," she said.

Quite apart from the fact that he was surely going to recognise her at school next week. But she was trying not to think about that.

"You want me to look through the phone book for every single Alice?" he asked. "What's your second name?"

That wouldn't help him either, since it was listed under her stepfather's name.

"You can contact me through Becky," she said. This would also raise the chances of the other guy calling Becky, so Alice felt she was doing her friend a favour.

"I might just do that." He gave her one last kiss goodbye, slow and lingering, still not putting his arms around her but just leaning down towards her. She could have kissed him forever.

But there was Jules, yanking her by the arm, dragging her out into the cool night which chilled her skin like a cold shower.

3. Bowled over

Alice was walking on air as they went through the streets to find a taxi. There was no point trying to get one in the throng spilling out of the Dog & Duck. The chances of getting into a cat fight or having someone vomit on your shoes were much higher.

"I think I'm in lust," she told them. "He kisses better than any guy I've ever known."

"You haven't kissed every guy you've ever known," Jules said.

But nothing could dampen Alice's spirits. Even with the alcohol wearing off she was in a buoyant mood.

Jules had to practically pull her out of the path of a car. "Have you taken something?" she asked.

"No, I'm just high on life."

"I wouldn't be if I were you. You won't be singing on Monday morning when he spots you in assembly. Or tomorrow morning given how much you've drunk."

They were all heading back to Jules' house. Her parents were the most laid back about them returning in the early hours. Becky's parents had no idea how late they stayed out.

Becky herself was also elated, gushing about her cricketer. "Brett's only twenty-two and his mum's a nurse just like mine."

"Come on, we'll go to the taxi rank in the High Street or we'll never make it home," Jules said. She was usually the party animal of the three so it was odd for her to be like this.

"Why are you on such a downer?" Alice asked. "Is it because you didn't pull?"

"I did pull if you must know. He asked for my number but he's not my type."

"He was nice looking," Becky said.

"It takes more than that. He was too wholesome."

The other two were in fits of laughter at this. "You play Captain Sensible all night and then you complain because the guy who hits on you is too wholesome? You were the one who set us all up with them."

Alice guessed that Jules was worried about Mr Walker. Jules was trying to stay out of trouble that term, the last thing she wanted was a suspension before their final exams. She'd got her dream offer to read law at one of the best universities in the country but she needed top results in her A-levels to take it up.

Not that she was the only one. Alice was hoping to do veterinary science which was even more competitive. Though she did have a few more options in front of her.

Her spirits were still soaring as they rode in the taxi. She felt warm and happy all over. A gorgeous man kissed me, she thought. An actual man. Not a schoolboy.

"Did Brett say when he'd call you?" she asked Becky. She hadn't given a lot of thought to what she would actually do if Mr Walker did try and contact her. She wanted him to, of course, but she had no idea where it could go if he did.

"No, but he said he'd call me for next weekend."

"Does he know you're still at school?" Alice asked.

"Yes but he didn't seem bothered by it."

Jules made a sarcastic noise from the front seat. "I don't think your Romeo will be quite so laid back, Alice."

"Maybe I could just avoid him at school all week. Make sure I don't go near the cricket pitches."

But there were a thousand places she could bump into him. Assembly. The dining hall. The main corridor past the staff room. Anywhere else in the grounds.

"Maybe you'd better just get it over with," Becky suggested. "Perhaps he'll be cool about it. After all, you are eighteen."

"He could get sacked, Becky. And we'd probably all get suspended or even expelled if they found out we were going about the town with fake ID and getting off with county cricketers," Jules said.

It was a strange thing being eighteen. In theory they were adults and could do what they liked. In practice there were a whole host of rules about upholding the school's reputation that they could still fall foul of.

"Your best bet," Jules continued, "is that he sees you, gets over his shock, and completely blanks you. Never refers to it again. It's not like you need to have any dealings with him, is it?"

This was true. But Alice wasn't sure she just wanted to forget about it.

They arrived at Jules' house, split the cost of the taxi fare, and crept inside as quietly as possible. Jules' parents - her father and stepmother - were pretty tolerant but they didn't want to push their luck.

"You're lucky having Kate you know," Alice said, referring to Jules' stepsister. Kate was the same age as them but she went to a different school.

"How so?"

"She's blazed the trail for you. She's always had loads of freedom so now your dad has to treat you the same."

Jules' father had remarried when she was fourteen, and though she didn't mind her stepmother she hadn't initially got on very well with Kate. They had resented one another badly at first and this had eventually progressed into a sort of blank tolerance. Only the last year or so had relations thawed. But both had entirely different interests, schools and friend groups so they didn't really socialise together.

Both Jules and Alice had lost a parent: Alice's father had been killed in a car accident before she was born, and Jules' mother died when Jules was eight. It was partly what had brought them together as friends.

"I don't think I'll ever shower again," Alice said as they brushed their teeth. "I want to feel the smell of him all over me."

"You won't say that when you wake up tomorrow reeking of stale booze and sweat."

Right now all Alice wanted to do was fall asleep and dream of Mr Walker. Once she was in bed she closed her eyes and relived the entire night, replaying the moment his lips touched hers over and over again. She didn't want the memory to fade. It still gave her a jolt in her stomach just to think about it.

If only he was here now, running his hands all over her body. She was still a virgin but she would definitely go all the way with him.

Right now the little voice saying "he's a teacher!" was well suppressed by the euphoria of it all.

* * *

The sun was horribly bright, Alice's head was splitting and her mouth was desert dry. Jules had been right: and even she had woken up feeling fairly rough. Becky just pulled the sheet over her head and moaned.

Despite her intentions of the previous night Alice went straight for the bathroom. Jules' parents had an amazingly powerful shower that drummed down on her, half punishment, half pleasure.

Closing her eyes in the steam she replayed everything that had happened. Much of it was hazy but she remembered the kissing, how she had felt, how much she wanted it again. And more.

Next week was going to be interesting, if he recognised her.

Back in Jules' bedroom there was a discussion going on about whether they should go to the cricket that day. "We could take your dad's pass and sit in the members' enclosure," Becky was saying.

Alice guessed that Becky, who had no interest in cricket, wanted to watch Brett play.

"God no, way too keen," she advised her. "Not unless he specifically asked you to come. Did he?"

Becky admitted that nothing had been said.

"He's going to call you, isn't he? Leave it at that."

"Alice is right you know," Jules agreed. "You don't want to look like a groupie."

"Does cricket have groupies?" Becky asked.

"Lawn bowls has groupies," Alice said. "Seriously. You don't want to be that girl. Let him pursue you."

"I bet you'd go if Mr Walker was going to be there," Becky said.

Alice's stomach flipped slightly at the prospect. There was a strong chance he would be there, given his friendship with Gloucestershire's coach. But she thought about it for a moment. "No, I wouldn't. Even if there wasn't the whole complication of him being at school next week I still wouldn't go. It'd just look sad."

"Besides which are they even playing at home?" Jules asked.

"In Taunton. But it's not far."

"No way can you go then, it will look absolutely desperate. Like you're stalking him."

Becky was obviously disappointed but she couldn't win against both of them. Nor did she want to go by herself. "What if he goes out tonight and meets someone else?"

"If he does, he does," Jules said. "They are sportsmen. What goes on tour and so on."

"I think he really liked you," Alice said, to console Becky who was now looking really glum. It wasn't exactly a lie, Alice couldn't honestly remember through the haze of lust and drink what Brett's intentions were or weren't. But she didn't want Becky making an idiot of herself or feeling miserable. "And they're not on tour anyway, they won't be staying overnight if it's only Somerset."

They were all going to sit around brooding if they didn't go out and do something. Alice suggested they go shopping. "You can look for something nice to wear for when he calls you," she said.

4. In the pavilion

Monday came all too soon. From the moment she stepped through the school gates Alice was on edge, anticipating that she might encounter Mr Walker at any moment.

Assembly was an absolute ordeal. She kept her head down and tried to hide in the crowd as she entered the hall. She deliberately avoided Becky and Jules, fearing they would be more recognisable as a threesome. To her relief Becky and Jules weren't sitting together either. Jules was late and had to take a seat nearer the front.

For all her worry Mr Walker didn't even appear in assembly that day. It wasn't completely mandatory for teachers and as a cricket coach he wasn't even full time.

At lunch they came up with a plan. "Biting the bullet is best," Jules had decided. "We'll go and watch the cricket after tennis and let him see you. Get this over with. Otherwise you'll just be distracted by it for days."

It was a beautiful late April day, flawlessly sunny. Warm in the sun though cool in the shade. Their tennis skirts were also extremely short and much more alluring, so Alice thought, than normal school uniform. You were supposed to wear huge regulation gym knickers underneath. But as these were only sold in the school shade of bottle green which looked awful through white tennis wear, no one ever did unless they were playing a match.

They walked together over to the school cricket pitch and sat on the grassy slope near the pavilion.

"He's going to freak you know," Jules said.

"Maybe he won't recognise her in different clothes."

"He'll recognise the three of us."

They watched the play for some time. Mr Walker was focused on his job and not on any spectators around the place. Alice was impressed by how athletic he looked as he walked about the pitch. He really was stunning with his tan and his tall, muscular figure. All the First Eleven boys looked wimpy next to him.

It was when he passed near to where they were sitting that he finally saw Alice, stopped and froze. Her stomach lurched. Then he turned away and went back to the practice.

"See, he's decided to ignore you," Jules said. "All for the best."

Alice said nothing. She hadn't really thought about how he might react, but she still felt crushed.

"Should we go?" Becky asked.

"No, that would look really weird, and besides Mike Jackson looks totally fit in cricket whites."

Mike captained the school cricket team and was one of the heartthrobs of Fairmount. But the problem with being in the Upper Sixth was that most girls preferred to date boys a year or so older. These were now long gone to university and the boys in their own year were in turn dating girls in lower years. Alice could also remember when Mike was several inches shorter than them and it detracted from his charms now.

"I wouldn't have thought Mike Jackson was your type," Becky said.

"He's not. Doesn't mean I can't enjoy looking, though. You know his older brother's playing for Worcestershire?"

"I don't remember him having an older brother."

"A few years before our time. Joe Jackson." Jules said.

Alice remained silent throughout this. She was still feeling disappointed and uncertain. She tried to tell herself it was for the best. Really, she should be grateful that he had just decided to move past it.

But she still felt embarrassed. She picked at the grass next to her, pulling off a small flower, avoiding looking at the play.

Then a shadow fell over them. She looked up.

It was Mr Walker.

"I want a word with you. In the pavilion, now," he ordered her. His eyes pierced into hers and he looked furious.

Numb, she obeyed, walking ahead of him.

Inside it was empty and he closed the door behind them and turned to her.

"What the fuck do you think you're playing at?"

He was absolutely incensed. He stood there, suddenly the adult, the authority, not just some guy she had kissed in a pub.

Someone she had compromised. Alice couldn't think of anything to say.

She stood there in front of him. His scent of faint cologne and sun-warmed skin was disturbingly familiar to her, mingling with the dusty wood and sports equipment smell of the pavilion.

"Did you know who I was?" he asked.

"Yes." There didn't seem to be any point in lying.

He glared at her and she looked back at him. His eyes pierced into her, their light grey-blue contrasting with his tanned complexion. He was one of the most devastatingly attractive men she had ever seen. All the more so now as his anger turned his face into carved steel.

As terrified and awkward as Alice felt, she also felt slightly defiant. After all she hadn't done anything wrong or illegal.

Then suddenly he grasped her by the shoulders and brought his mouth down on hers, hard. Surprised, she initially squirmed to escape his grasp then yielded as her forced his tongue into her mouth. His lips were bruising hers, he was almost biting her yet she wanted more.

Her hands, which had pushed against his chest to try and get away, went round his neck and she arched against him.

He was trying to hurt her, devour her. Punish her. All at once. But he wanted her too. She could taste his need, raw and urgent. Feel the hotness of his breath as he nearly suffocated her with his kiss.

His mouth left hers and moved to her neck, half embracing, half biting it. She tasted blood on her lip where he had crushed it with his own. He was gripping her hard and she clung to him. She didn't even care that he was hurting her.

He could have ripped all her clothes off right there and forced himself upon her. She had never wanted anyone so much.

Then just as suddenly he thrust her away from him. He swore under his breath as he tried to recover himself.

"Is that what you wanted?"

"No... yes... I mean..." Alice had no idea what to say. She was shaken and half in misery, half in ecstasy.

His face was like granite, its angles unyielding.

"Get out and don't come back here again. Stay out of my way," he said.

Too stunned to respond Alice went out. She thought she heard him mutter something about "jailbait" as she left.

Outside, still sitting on the grass, Jules and Becky were agog to know what had gone on.

"What the hell happened in there?" Jules saw Alice's bleeding lip. "Oh god, did he hit you?"

"No, of course not." Alice involuntarily put a hand on her neck, which drew Jules' attention to it. She grabbed Alice's hand away.

"You have a love bite on your neck? What the hell?"

"Let's just get out of here," Alice said. She wanted to get away. She couldn't face his anger or contempt any longer.

"Okay, but you'd better tell us exactly what's going on."

"Nothing's going on," Alice said as they got up and walked back to the main school. She couldn't even bring herself to look behind her and see where he was.

"He summons you into the pavilion and you come out moments later with a bleeding lip and an enormous love bite and that's nothing?" Jules was incredulous.

"How are you going to cover that?" Becky asked. "You can hardly wear a scarf in May. And your collar won't go anywhere near it."

"I don't know, a Band-Aid." It was the last thing on Alice's mind.

"You can't wear a Band-Aid on your neck, everyone will know exactly what it's concealing."

"Forget about concealing the bloody love bite, Becky. How it happened is more to the point," Jules said.

"He was angry, and then he kissed me, and then he was angry again."

"Jesus!"

"Are you ok, Alice?" Becky asked.

"Yeah, I'm fine. Well no I'm not fine, I don't really know what I am, but I'm ok," Alice said. She was absolutely confused. How she felt about him, how he felt about her, what any of this meant, what she was going to do. It was like he hated her but wanted her at the same time.

Again and again she re-ran it in her mind, every second, every sensation. She wanted his hunger and even the pain again, his anger. She imagined it dissolving into something more sensuous as their embrace continued. He couldn't maintain that level of rage for long. Or could he?

* * *

Becky was thrilled when Brett rang her on Monday night. She'd been suffering silently as well, hoping and hoping that he'd call her and that he hadn't lost her number.

She told the others the next morning as they filed into Assembly. "There's a barbecue at some guy's house on Sunday. Loads of the players are going. We're all invited."

"I can't go," Jules said. "Kate's invited me to this thing in Lechlade over the weekend, some sort of festival at a quarry."

"Doesn't sound like your sort of thing," Alice said. Jules' stepsister's friends were much more crusty than they were. They went to folk festivals and eco protests.

"I said I'd give it a go." Now Jules and Kate would soon be going their separate ways at university it had defused some of the tensions between them.

"What about the cinema on Sunday night, can you still make it?" They were planning to see Basic Instinct which had finally been released in the UK.

"Sure, I'll meet you there."

"What about you Alice? I can't go by myself to the barbecue. They're expecting a group of us," Becky said.

Alice was in two minds. On one hand she wanted to support Becky, but the thought of seeing all the cricketers again just reminded her of her humiliation with Mr Walker.

But if the roles were reversed she would have been desperate for Becky to support her. "Okay, I'll come," she said.

Becky was so profusely grateful that Alice felt bad for having wavered.

As they entered the Assembly hall Alice fought with herself not to look around for Mr Walker. In the end she lost her nerve and kept her head down.

"Mr Walker's here," Becky whispered to her so loudly that Alice thought he'd hear them from the far side of the room. She felt herself go red and tried to stoop down and hide even more. "He is really good looking isn't he?" Becky continued. She was saying it to return the favour to Alice as Alice was supporting her with Brett. Though it was undeniably true.

Alice couldn't help looking up and across at the cricket coach. His eyes met her for a split second, his expression unreadable, and then he turned abruptly.

"He's looking at you Alice!" Becky said.

"Shut up Becky. She's not blind and half the school can hear you."

Becky looked crushed but buttoned her lip.

Alice could only see Mr Walker from the back now as he went to the seating area at the reserved for staff. He was tall with amazing shoulders, the back of his head perfectly sculpted. She forced herself to sit down and face the stage, so he wouldn't see her looking at him when he turned round again.

All through Assembly she could feel his eyes burning into the back of her head. She tried to tell herself that he probably wasn't even looking at her.

Becky couldn't resist twisting her head round to see. "I can't tell if he's watching you but he looks really serious," she said, managing to whisper this time.

Jules could still hear her. "Stop looking around. He's already pissed off enough."

Alice wondered how he actually felt. Angry? Embarrassed? Disappointed? Maybe he had been really intending to call her before he discovered her real age?

She bitterly regretted having let him find out. Perhaps she could have hidden from him for at least another week at school and maybe gone on one date with him. Though that might have made it even worse when he did finally realise.

What's done is done, she thought. She wondered whether it was her age or being at the same school that bothered him most. Both probably.

5. Considerations

Wednesday was a half day at school. The younger pupils had organised activities after lunch ranging from cadet force to various clubs and volunteer programmes. The Sixth Formers were left to their own devices so unless they had a match to play they were free to leave school after lunch. Often they snuck away before lunch but there was a risk of detention if you got caught.

Alice had a part-time job at a local veterinary practice. It had reaffirmed her desire to work with animals but also made her realise she didn't want to be a small animal vet. The problem wasn't the animals, it was the owners. Too many pets got put down because someone didn't want to pay for an animal to be treated. She also hated seeing supposedly loving owners mistreat or neglect their animals. Anything from failing to give them medication properly, feed them properly or get their claws clipped on a regular basis.

But seeing a sick animal gradually get better each week, and the owner's growing relief and joy, that was wonderful. It made it all worthwhile.

Exotic pet owners tended to be among the better owners as they were more invested in their animals. The first patient that day was a lizard with a severe calcium deficiency. The man bringing it in had recently bought it from a pet shop in a nearby town.

"I could tell it was sick when I bought it but they just didn't care. I couldn't let it die," he told them. He owned several other reptiles and was experienced in their care.

The vet, a woman about ten years older than Alice, prescribed a course of calcium injections and supplements and ensured the lizard had access to proper UV-B lighting.

"Yeah, that's no problem," the man said. He looked to be in his late thirties, scruffy with long hair and a stubble that was nearly a beard, but he clearly cared about his animals. "I've got an empty habitat all set up."

The vet also took the name of the pet shop. The man had already reported it to animal welfare but she liked to make her own investigations. The practice kept a blacklist of problem pet shops and breeders and cooperated with prosecutions when necessary.

The man held the lizard when it was injected. Usually Alice did this but experienced owners could generally be trusted to hold their pets firmly enough and it kept the animals calmer. It was actually the thing she'd found hardest at first: keeping the animal still without hurting it. "You can nearly always hold them much more firmly than you think," Jo, the vet, had told her. "Better that than they flip out and jump off the table with a needle in them."

Alice and Jo had become quite friendly over the couple of years that Alice had worked there. Jo was impressed that Alice was serious about becoming a vet and had written her letters of recommendation as well as lending her various books and veterinary journals.

Jo also hated selfish owners. She had even kept alive a litter of kittens when someone brought in a heavily pregnant cat and wanted the pregnancy terminated. "It's only about a day from giving birth," she told Alice and the veterinary nurses that worked there.

They had had to keep the four kittens alive around the clock for the first weeks, each taking a kitten and doing their best as the mother cat was now back with its callous owner. It had been an eye opening experience for Alice, feeding her kitten every few hours with a syringe and special formula. Happily they had all survived and homes had been found for them. One of the nurses had taken two.

Owners like that were a strong reason why Jo was thinking of giving up the practice. Her fiancé was South African and there was a possibility they might relocate there.

"Won't you find it hard to leave all your friends and family and move so far away?" Alice had asked her.

"Yes, but being with Pieter makes up for it. And I'd love the chance to work in a wildlife sanctuary over there," Jo had said.

Jo's future move had influenced Alice's own travel plans with Jules. She had been researching wildlife organisations in South East Asia where you could volunteer. Alice planned to write to some of them in advance. Jules's travel plans were more beach-and-party oriented, but Alice wanted to do something worthwhile if she could.

Alice had originally hoped Becky would come with them, but she hadn't been interested. Becky didn't like the idea of roughing it at backpackers' hostels and wanted to start physiotherapy straight away. She came from a medical family - father a GP, mother a nurse - and was more of a home town girl. She had only applied to physiotherapy courses within an hour's radius of their town.

Alice's mother hadn't initially been in favour of her taking a gap year. "Vet science is such a long course, darling, don't you think it would be better to get it underway?" But Alice wanted a break before she threw herself into it. It was going to be even more intensive than school, and once she graduated she'd have to find work rather than be free to travel.

Only Alice's stepfather Richard had understood. "Travel can be a very educational experience," he said. "It may give you perspective on your own future path."

* * *

Everyone was out except Richard when Alice got home. Her mother was taking her younger brothers to swimming club so the house was quiet.

Alice always felt she'd struck lucky getting Richard as a stepfather. She held no resentment towards him for taking her father's place. After all, she'd never known her father. He was just a nice looking man with seventies hair in the wedding photos her mother kept in a drawer.

Richard was more like a godfather than a stepfather, Alice thought. He was a quiet, scholarly man who was quite a few years older than her mother. He had been some sort of old family acquaintance and Alice's mother had married him when Alice was ten. In the next couple of years two little brothers came into Alice's life, both turning out to be well-behaved and serious like their father.

Having heard some of the stepfamily horror stories of her friends, including Jules and her early battles with Kate, Alice considered herself fortunate.

She stopped by his study. Other people's parents had home offices, but Richard had a study.

"Back from work?" he asked.

"Yes. Mainly cats and dogs, but we did get a very fat rabbit and a bearded dragon. Pogona vitticeps." Alice had looked up the Latin name in one of Jo's books. "Have you had supper?" Richard often forgot to eat if he was by himself, lost in his work.

"Your mother said something about bringing fish and chips home." This was good, since Alice hadn't eaten either.

"Richard, I was wondering about something," she began. She always called him by his first name, never Dad or Father.

He waited patiently for her to continue. He never hurried them out, he always made time for all of them no matter how busy he seemed to be.

"You and my mother. Was the age gap ever a problem?" There were twelve years between them.

Richard considered the question. "No, I can't say it was, not from my side. We were both adults with life experience. You might have to ask your mother for her view."

Alice liked how he took her seriously. "When you say life experience, would it be different if she had been my age?" she asked.

"Your mother was already a widow with a child. So yes, I expect it would have been a different situation if she was at an earlier stage of her life." He didn't ask her why she was asking this which Alice was grateful for. Her mother would have instantly freaked out and assumed Alice had some unsuitable boyfriend who was taking advantage of her.

Which wasn't the case at all. But Alice rather wished it was.

* * *

Alice sat in her bedroom. Something about it seemed different, but she wasn't sure why. She looked around the room. Her corkboard was covered with photos: of her family, of Jules, Becky and her doing various things.

There was a poster of some pop star on the wall by her bed. Jules had cut it out of a magazine and stuck it up as a joke. Alice had left it up because she secretly found him attractive, but now she took it down. The Blu-Tack left marks on the paint when she picked it off. She would have to put something else there to cover it.

There were also some things on her dresser that an ex boyfriend had given her. She wasn't sure if they held sentimental value or not, it had been an amicable split. But seized by an urge to clear things away, she found a shoebox and packed them into it.

A stuffed toy won at a fair. A friendship bracelet. A couple of beermats. She couldn't even remember the night they were from or their significance.

She didn't want to put all her childhood things away, but she wanted less clutter. If it wasn't for the fact that she was leaving to go travelling soon, and then university, she would have asked her mother if she could redecorate. Except she wasn't sure what she really wanted to change.

Some things would come with her, of course, to furnish whatever student accommodation she ended up in. Pretty much nothing would go backpacking with her. She and Jules were competing to take the least amount of gear so they could travel as light as possible and bring back more souvenirs at the end.

Souvenirs that would probably never end up here. She was leaving this room behind. It would still be hers, she didn't imagine Richard and her mother would take on a lodger, and the boys were quite happy with their rooms. But it would be her old room. It wouldn't quite be hers in the same way any more, even if it was kept for her.

Alice felt a pang of nostalgia: for her childhood, for the early days when it was just her mother and her, for Christmas and Easter with grandparents who were now dead. For the safety of it all, for the comfort. Despite not having her father she had enjoyed a very happy time growing up.

Of course she hadn't thought of it as easy at the time, who does? She had just taken it all for granted, but it had been easy. Compared with the future which at times seemed terrifying. Terrifying, but exciting as well.

6. The barbecue

Having buried herself in schoolwork that week and after revising most of Saturday, Sunday came as a relief. It dawned clear and sunny, holding all the hope and promise of a beautiful English summer. Of course the chances of another poor, rainy year were no worse than any other year but there was something about the start of summer that made everyone joyful. It hadn't failed yet.

It was warm enough for summer clothes so Alice wore a white vest and jeans. A sundress seemed a bit too much in May, particularly for a barbecue.

Becky picked her up. She had deliberately chosen to drive so she couldn't drink too much. She was incredibly nervous about seeing Brett again.

"Thanks so much for coming, I couldn't have gone by myself, not knowing anyone else there."

Alice was glad she had been persuaded into going as it was such a nice day. She read the map and they made their way to a house in a village a few miles out of town. Cars were parked on both sides of the road and up the driveway which ran alongside the house. They could hear voices and smell barbecue smoke so they walked around the side instead of knocking on the front door.

Happily for Becky, Brett was already there. He greeted her with a kiss and put his arm around her. Becky did look very pretty that day. She was a petite girl with dark, wavy hair. She was wearing a lacy blouse and new white jeans. Alice felt a bit casual next to her but everyone else there was in regular jeans and t-shirts. She saw the red-haired guy who had chatted up Jules, his name was Graeme, and Grant, the other Australian.

And then she saw him. Mr Walker, holding a beer, talking with Chris.

He saw her and his face turned to stone.

Alice honestly had had no idea he would be here. She hadn't even considered it. From what Becky had said she just assumed it would be all the younger guys, the players. Surely they didn't hang out with their coach all the time?

Becky was so enraptured with Brett who had taken her off to one side that she didn't even notice.

"Hello, it's jailbait again," Graeme said, coming over and handing her a beer. So they all knew. She was mortified. Her face showed it.

"We've all been giving him a hard time. Don't worry, he'll get over it. Just don't call him Headmaster," Graeme warned.

"You haven't been calling him that?"

Graeme grinned. "Yes. And he's furious. He also had no idea you were coming along."

Alice felt like she'd been set up. "I didn't know he'd be here either."

"Would you have stayed away if you had?"

The answer to this was probably no, quite the reverse, but Alice couldn't admit it. "I just came for Becky. She was worried about finding the place by herself.

"Well don't worry, I'll look after you. I see your other friend has jilted me."

He meant Jules. "She had to go to some festival."

"A rave?" Graeme asked.

"Maybe, some sort of hippy thing. Near Lechlade."

"She didn't look the type for that."

"She's not, it was her sister's idea," Alice told him.

"The Australians are desperate to go to a rave. They heard all about them before they came. Let us know if you're going to any."

Alice didn't go to that many raves but she promised she'd let Graeme know if there were any happening. Kate would know if anyone. "They're always last minute though and sometimes hard to find in the dark." She remembered how horribly lost they had got the last time they'd tried to find one. After driving for ages in apparent circles around unlit country lanes on a moonless night, they'd finally found the location. Only to discover the police had got there about fifteen minutes earlier and were already breaking it up.

Alice tried to enjoy herself at the barbecue but she couldn't relax with Mr Walker just metres away, deliberately avoiding her. She had no appetite but knew she needed to eat something to avoid getting completely drunk on an empty stomach.

Graeme was good company and buoyed up by misery, alcohol and perhaps a desire to make a point to Mr Walker she flirted with him a bit. He was the kind of guy you could flirt with without it meaning much. Besides she knew he preferred Jules. She also noticed that Mr Walker's gaze was frequently on her and he didn't look happy about her flirting with Graeme. Or she hoped that was why he looked annoyed.

As the beer went down the revelry increased and someone accidentally knocked a glass full of beer over Alice. It went all over her top.

Feeling as though nothing much more could go wrong with the day she found her way to the kitchen and tried to sponge out the worst at the sink. If the beer dried on it, it would smell awful and probably stain the fabric. Hopefully even though she was getting her top even more wet it would dry quickly in the sun.

As she was finishing getting the worst off someone else came into the kitchen. She knew even before she turned that it was Mr Walker. He looked angry.

"Did you come here deliberately?" he asked.

She faced him. "I came here with Becky. I didn't know you'd be here. Or care," she added.

"What have you done to your shirt?"

"Someone spilt beer on it. I was washing it off."

"You can't go back out like that. You look like a wet t-shirt competition," he told her.

Alice looked down and went red. The wet fabric had gone transparent and soaked through her bra too.

Without a word Mr Walker pulled off his own shirt and handed it to her. He wore nothing under it. Alice was transfixed by his physique. His arms rippled with muscle and his flat, hard chest was tanned a deep gold. He was far fitter than she expected a cricketer to be, really powerful looking.

"Put this on."

The shirt was white cotton and warm from his body. She held it. It smelt of him. She wanted to envelop herself in it but she didn't follow his order.

"You want me to walk out of here wearing your shirt with you following me, topless?" she asked him.

He was silent for a moment, glaring at her. She was right, it would have exactly the opposite effect he intended. The situation was bad enough as it was.

"I don't want them gawping at you."

Alice's stomach gave a secret flip. Possessive and protective. He clearly didn't feel as neutrally towards her as he wanted to.

"The sun will dry it. I'll cross my arms." As she said this, she deliberately left her arms uncrossed and put her shoulders back slightly.

It had the desired effect. He was momentarily transfixed.

"Jesus Christ."

Alice took charge of the situation. "You should put this back on." Instead of just handing it to him she went to put it over his head meaning her arms were raised and her body was nearly against his. He was still for a second before taking a step backwards. A muscle clenched in his jaw.

"Just give me the shirt." She did so and he put it back on.

Then they both stood there. The tension was unbearable. She knew he wanted her and was fighting against it with every fibre of his being.

She broke the ice. "I am sorry you know. We were all just having fun the other night and I just didn't think about the implications."

"You were just messing around with me because I'm employed at your school?"

"God no, that wasn't why." Alice couldn't believe he thought this. Surely he'd realised how much she also wanted him to kiss her that night?

"So even if I hadn't been, you would have still put on your little act?" he asked.

What act? "I wasn't acting, I genuinely..."

"You wanted it too?"

"Yes." It was barely a whisper.

For a moment she thought he was going to kiss her again. He was wavering. Then he stood straighter. "I'm way too old for you, Alice, and I work at your school. Get back outside."

Alice felt half dejected, half victorious when she walked back out into the garden. At least she knew he liked her. He had revealed far more than he had intended. She just needed to break down his defences a bit more.

Becky hadn't even noticed her absence. Graeme had, and gave her a sly grin.

"You were inside a while with Stewie. Took a shower together did you?" he said noticing her wet shirt.

"Nothing is happening. He's still mad."

"He's too old for you anyway."

Fed up with hearing this and wanting to change the subject, Alice asked Graeme if he'd been to school in the area.

"Yeah, Northlands Hall. Over Stroud way."

It was where Kate went. "I know it. Jules's sister goes there. I doubt you'd know her though."

"It's six years since I left, so probably not."

Six years. That made him around twenty-four. Alice found herself wondering again how old Mr Walker was. If only he'd been an England player she could have looked him up in Jules' father's Cricketers' Who's Who. Was there an Australian version? Maybe Brett would know how old he was. He must be about the same age as Chris and that would be easier to find out.

She realised she had fallen for him. She also realised it would be wisest to stay away. She hardly needed this kind of distraction in her A-level term. She had to do well or she'd be letting Jules down if the backpacking got cancelled.

7. Basic Instinct

Jules was wearing a pair of tie-dye harem pants when they caught up with her that evening outside the cinema.

"What the hell are those?" Alice asked.

"I got them at the festival, they're really comfy."

"They're lurid. And they smell of weed. And patchouli. Or you do, anyway."

Jules shrugged. "I didn't have time to shower."

"More like you didn't dare go home smelling like that." They were staying at Becky's house tonight. Jules' parents might be more laid back than average but they weren't that tolerant.

"Where's Kate?" Becky asked. "Didn't she want to come?"

"She's staying with friends around Cirencester somewhere."

"Was it good?"

"It was amazing. Thousands of people. It was in this quarry and they put up a big top. It cost to get in but it was worth it. We stayed up dancing all night and in the morning it was really beautiful, all misty over the lake," Jules said.

Alice felt envious. "Let us know when the next one is, if Kate gets a tip off. Graeme said some of the players want to go."

They went in to see the film which had caused such a sensation in the US and came out arguing about the ending.

"It was definitely her, she had the ice pick under her bed," Alice said.

"I think that was a twist. Another bluff."

"I thought it was horrible," Becky said. "She was so awful and there was all that sex and death."

"That was kind of the point of it, Becky. It was an erotic thriller," Jules told her.

Becky was glad she hadn't seen the film with Brett as she would have been incredibly embarrassed. He wasn't able to meet her that night because there was some kind of team event on. So the three of them were going for pizza and possibly a pub and then back to Becky's house.

"We'll never get into anywhere nice with your hippy trousers," Alice said.

"Let's just go and eat then. I'm hungry and quite tired and Becky's only going to be mooning about her cricketer."

"Alice too. Mr Walker was there today."

Jules turned on Alice. "You never told me that."

"I didn't get a chance," Alice said. "Besides it wasn't relevant. I didn't even know he would be there."

"So nothing happened?"

Alice hesitated. Nothing had really happened, and she didn't want another lecture from Jules.

But it was too late of for that. "So something did happen?"

"We got into a bit of a row."

"The lads have all been calling him Headmaster," Becky told Jules. "It's really funny, he got so annoyed."

They had reached a pizza chain restaurant and went inside to get a table. It was busy inside despite being a Sunday night, but Jules simply went up to a table by the window and took off the reserved sign. They always did this and they always got away with it. It wasn't as though there were any VIPs or celebrities in town.

"What was the row about?" Jules asked Alice.

Alice explained as briefly as she could. Jules started laughing. "OK I give up. Do what you will. The pair of you are idiots."

"Nothing happened, we didn't do anything idiotic or not."

"For God's sake, Alice, he's a grown man ripping his shirt off and playing Mr Chivalry, and then blowing you off right afterwards. He obviously likes you. And he's obviously got minimal self-control. Just go for it if you're that into him," Jules said.

"So I've got your green light?"

"Yes. Anyway given what I got up to I'm hardly in a position to play Senior Mistress." The Senior Mistress at Fairmount was a Mrs Paddington, a dour widow in her late fifties who was responsible for behaviour and discipline.

"That's good because you were starting to remind me of the Padlock. So spill the beans on your weekend."

They bickered as usual over the pizza toppings and what kind of crust to get. Becky hated anchovies, Alice hated pineapple and Jules usually hated everything except pepperoni. Tonight Jules was so hungry she gave way and they ended up with ham and mushroom.

"I thought you couldn't stand mushrooms?" Becky said.

"I can't usually. But I'm giving them another chance. I had some mushroom tea earlier and it was lovely."

"That's not all you had, judging by the smell," Alice said.

"My parents will think it's woodsmoke. Or I'll just wash my clothes out."

* * *

Becky's house was always immaculately neat and tidy, including her bedroom which put the others to shame. The whole family were medically inclined: as well as her doctor-nurse parents she had an older sister in her final year of nursing and a brother who had just started pharmacology.

Jules washed her clothes with shampoo in the basin and hung them over the radiator to dry. "I'll tell your mum I spilt coke on them," she told Becky.

"What happened to your own clothes?" Becky asked.

"No idea."

Something more was going on with Jules, Alice thought. Given how strait-laced she'd been so far this term, this sudden descent into hedonism on the cusp of their exams had to have some other reason. Jules was not the sort of person to get high all day in the middle of final classes and revision. Either she was having some kind of a crisis or there was a guy involved. Alice thought the latter was most likely.

"So did you meet anyone there?" she asked.

"Maybe."

Becky was instantly excited. "Who? What's he like?"

"There was this guy, he's a tree surgeon. And an environmentalist."

"You mean an eco-warrior?" Alice asked.

"No, not really. I mean he wouldn't want it described like that."

"So what's his name? Twig or Moss or something?" Jules looked embarrassed. "Oh god it is, isn't it? He's got one of those crusty tree hugging names."

"His name's Ben."

"But he's not called that, is he? You'd better tell us or if we meet him we're going to laugh."

"Some of the people call him Leafy."

This was pure gold. "So you're going to be a high profile corporate lawyer with a crusty boyfriend called Leafy?"

"No. I don't even know if I want to do that any more."

"You mean not do law? Your father would kill you," Alice said.

"I mean not that kind of law," Jules said. "I don't know."

"It seems pretty sudden, changing your mind in just one day."

"It wasn't just one day, I've been thinking about it for a while." Jules looked unhappy.

Alice felt a pang of alarm. If Jules suddenly went off the rails and failed her exams it could disrupt their travel plans. Jules' trip was partly dependent on some money her father had promised her if she got top grades. Alice had saved up enough from her vet job to pay for her own side.

Becky's bedroom had twin beds with frilly valances and a white dressing table with gilded handles. It was the kind of room Alice longed for as a child but had grown out of now. They always flipped a coin to decide whether she or Jules got the mattress on the floor or the other bed. Alice had won that night.

Pillows and sheets and duvets were sorted out and they got ready for bed. Jules was grumbling about ending up with the blow-up mattress.

"You'll have to get used to that with Leafy," Alice said. "He probably sleeps on the ground."

"They have vans. With proper beds."

"A caravan isn't my idea of a proper bed. We went caravanning once and it was awful," Becky said. "Really narrow and cramped. But it's the lavatories that are the worst."

"How does that happen?" Alice asked.

"They bury it. It's all very clean," Jules told her. Alice imagined trying to dig a trench with a shovel by moonlight. She hoped their backpacking trip wouldn't involve too much of that.

"Do they sleep in pyjamas?" Becky asked.

"No, I don't know, maybe." Jules was getting exasperated. "We were up all night so I didn't really pay much attention to the sleeping arrangements."

"Tie dye pyjamas."

"Crack pipe and slippers."

Jules was getting annoyed now so Alice thought she had better change the subject. "Do you realise it's just six weeks?"

"Six weeks what?"

"Six weeks until we're done with Fairmount. Forever."

"It'll be a bit sad, don't you think?" Becky said.

"It will be amazing. No more Padlock. No more school food. No more Maddy Pullen." Maddy, Jules' sworn enemy, was one of the in crowd at school. All the boys liked her, and she her friends were usually bitchy to everyone else.

"I will be glad to see the back of her," Alice agreed.

"In the film, that scene with his girlfriend, was that rape?" Becky asked. She was still thinking about Basic Instinct.

Jules didn't know. "I think it was maybe just more heated. Like in the heat of the moment."

"Do guys like that? I don't think I would," Becky said.

Alice didn't think she had much to worry about with Brett in that regard. He looked more like a puppy dog than a stallion. Her thoughts went to Mr Walker, momentarily casting herself in the scene with him. Given the savage way he had kissed her in the pavilion she could well imagine him doing something like that. Grabbing her from behind and having his way with her. She shivered.

Lying in bed she imagined a different outcome at the barbecue. What if his resolve and faltered and he had ripped her t-shirt off and covered her body with his?

She imagined his hands on her breasts, his rock hard body crushing hers. Would he stand up and take her against the wall, or bend her over like Basic Instinct? Or would he throw her down on the tiles, push her legs apart and make her his?

She wanted him so badly it was nearly painful. Her body felt neglected. She couldn't remember ever having desired anyone else this badly. She'd dated boys before and they'd messed around, but she'd never felt an overwhelming urge to just lose all her inhibitions and better judgement and go all the way.

At least she had a kind of non-school link to him through Becky now, if there were any more group social occasions like that. At some point surely his resistance would break down? Particularly as the end of term approached, removing those concerns.

8. School tensions

Alice felt differently at school the next week. Knowing that Mr Walker liked her and was fighting his attraction to her gave her an illicit thrill. Their paths didn't have much occasion to cross, as out of respect to his order she avoided the cricket pitches, but she noticed that he was in Assembly every morning and in lunch every day.

Nearly always she would find him looking at her, then deliberately looking away.

Jules had also finally decided to embrace the situation which made Alice feel better about things. Not that there was a situation, yet anyway, but Alice could feel something drawing them together like a magnet.

Beyond that, revision occupied most of their time. They mainly studied different subjects, only sharing a few subjects and none between all three of them. Alice had Economics with Jules so they revised together. She had Biology with Becky, who in turn had History with Jules.

On Wednesday the lizard and its owner were back at the vet, to Alice's relief it looked much better. She got to hold it this time, feeling the soft, dry warmth of its belly compared to the hard tough scales on its back. Reptiles would be an interesting area of practice.

On Thursday afternoon they had tennis and were once again in their micro skirts, aimlessly hitting balls over the net.

"What's the point of this?" said Jules. "None of us are on the tennis team, we leave forever in a matter of weeks, and we could use this time so much better for revision."

The games mistress gave some pat response about healthy bodies and healthy minds.

Jules was also annoyed because she'd had to partner with Maddy Pullen.

"I can vote, marry, drive a car and even join the army yet I'm still forced to play tennis twice a week." What Jules actually wanted to do was slip off that afternoon because there was a fair in town and Leafy would be there.

"Why would he be at a fair?" Becky asked.

"It's the fairground workers moving from place to place, it's like a travelling market."

Becky was confused. "You can't buy anything there except candyfloss and stuffed toys."

"Yes you can, if you know what you're buying," Jules told her.

Alice was staying as sober as possible that term, trying to drink less and avoid recreational substances. As tempting as it was to take her mind off all the exam stress, it probably wouldn't help her results.

She was worried about the influence of Kate and her friends on Jules. Kate had plans to do something like art or fashion and had half-heartedly applied to St Martins and a few other places but didn't have many offers. She was considering travelling for a year. Not backpacking like Alice and Jules intended, but joining the travelling community in the UK for a while.

Jules' parents would freak out, Alice thought, if she abandoned her plans to do law. She was also concerned that

Jules might change her mind about backpacking in Asia with her and go travelling with Kate and some convoy of crusties instead. But there wasn't a lot she could do if Jules did decide that.

After tennis they lazed about under the trees for a while as the weather was so good. No one felt like dusty classrooms and books.

"It's such a waste having exams in the summer term. They should be in winter when there's nothing to do except stay indoors and study," Alice said.

She stood up and grasped onto the branch of a tree, hanging off it for a moment and enjoying the stretch through her body.

"That's making your skirt ride up showing your knickers," Becky said.

Alice dropped down, not really caring until she looked across and saw Mr Walker about ten yards away. He would have clearly seen everything. She went scarlet.

"Nice one, putting on a show for your man," Jules said.

"Do you think he saw?"

"I shouldn't think so. Assuming he's registered blind, and shut his eyes, and was facing the other way."

Alice buried her face in her hands.

"He just looked over again," Becky told her. "I think he was smiling."

* * *

Alice was looking after her younger brothers on Friday night because Richard and her mother were going out to a dinner party. They never expected her to babysit but she was usually happy to. They were good little boys. She sometimes wished she had a sibling nearer her own age but that was just one of the many dreams ended by her father's death.

She sat in her mother's bedroom, looking at the photos of him in the dressing table drawer while her mother chose earrings and finished her make up.

"Do you still think about him often?"

"Every day, when I see you. You have his eyes."

Alice felt bad but her mother reassured her.

"It's not a sad feeling any more, the way it used to be," she continued. "Of course it is sad, if I think about it in a certain way, but mainly I think about how proud of you he would have been. It's not the loss of him that hurts now but what he lost by never knowing you. And what you've lost."

"I feel guilty that I don't feel it," Alice said. "I try to, but it's like it happened to someone else."

"You weren't even born darling. You couldn't be expected to feel it in the same way as if you had known him."

Her mother was deciding between some diamanté drops and some pearls. "The pearls," Alice said. She liked that her mother's jewellery was discreet and elegant. She was never embarrassed by her mother like some girls were by theirs. She remembered an unfortunate classmate whose newly divorced mother had turned up blind drunk to the school concert and had flung herself at the chemistry teacher.

"With Richard, did it worry you that he was older?" she asked.

Alice's mother laughed. "Hardly. He was only in his forties and I was a grown woman with a child. If anything I felt very lucky that he felt that such a nice man had feelings for me. Enough men his age were casting their wives aside for a secretary half their age."

Alice, who considered her mother to be very beautiful, personally thought that Richard had got the better end of the deal but didn't say so. Although she liked Richard very much he wasn't an obvious Casanova. Or Lothario. Or whatever the men that went off with their secretaries were supposed to be.

"If I ended up with an older boy - a man - would you be very worried?" she asked.

"I'd be very upset if I thought someone was taking advantage of you. But if you met a nice man, and he was kind to you, then a few years difference wouldn't matter. I hope you'll finish your studies first though."

"I hope I won't be single for the next six years," Alice said.

"I mean in terms of settling down. You have so much time ahead of you." Her mother had finished blotting her lipstick and was getting up to leave.

"But you wouldn't mind if there was someone?"

"As long as you respect yourself and others, and be safe and careful, then you'll be alright." Her mother probably thought she was talking about her trip with Jules.

The boys were wildly excited as usual to have a night alone with Alice. She always spoiled them. They had already had their supper and bath early but she always let them have ice cream and stay up later than usual watching cartoons. The day would come soon enough when they would be awkward adolescents and not sweet little boys any more, she thought.

Alice envied them their companionship. Perhaps they'd fight later on, but for now they were like a little team, the best of friends. After they had gone to bed following extra stories and tucking in she felt lonely. She knew Jules was out with Leafy again but Becky was probably in. She rang her.

"I'm babysitting the boys. Do you want to come over?"

Becky was only a few minutes drive away. She was keen to see Alice so she could analyse and scrutinise how things were going with Brett. Jules had been a bit dismissive recently.

It was an interesting thing, being in a threesome of best friends. In such a group normally one person always got left out but somehow they made it work. There was a different type of glue for each of them. Alice and Jules were more academically similar: higher achieving and more ambitious, and had both lost parents. While their families were quite different, both were stepfamilies.

Jules and Becky had known each other since they were at playschool and their mothers had been friends. There was something that the two of them shared that felt alien to Alice but she could never put her finger on what it was. It didn't matter, it was just that on the surface of it Jules and Becky were the most different of all of them, with Jules being outspoken and confrontational and Becky being much quieter and more timid and conventional. One might expect Alice to get caught in between them but she rarely did.

Maybe the differences were the very thing that connected them. Becky grounded Jules while Jules pushed Becky out of her fear zone.

Alice and Becky both planned to work in medical fields and were less confrontational than Jules. They were the laid back ones, the ones who shared an eye roll when Jules once again got fired up about something.

Though recently Alice found herself feeling more rebellious and impatient, more like she thought Jules must feel. Everything felt like they were in limbo, they were hovering, waiting for something. She wanted it to come to fruition, whatever it was. Yet she feared even more that it might not do so, that she might have to chart her own course out of this and there would be no clear guides to point the way.

Becky arrived and as there was nothing on TV they made brownies. Becky was the most domestic of them and was a competent cook. Alice and Jules, fearing starvation if they went to university with no culinary skills, had started working their way through a "Cheap Meals for Students" recipe book that Jules' stepmother had given her. Every other recipe seemed to involve canned tuna, rice, beans or a combination of them.

"How did you pick all this up?" Alice asked Becky, licking the spoon while they waited for the brownies to cook.

"Mum taught me. We just always did it, since we were small. Even my brother."

"It makes me feel useless, I can barely boil potatoes," Alice said. She'd also burnt potatoes several times, letting them boil dry while she got distracted doing something else. "So how are things with Brett?" she asked, being generous as she knew Becky would want to talk her ear off.

"He's so wonderful! Honestly we have so much in common. I know it hasn't been long but I really haven't felt like this about anyone before." Becky continued to reel off Brett's wonders and Alice listened kindly, her mind wandering to other things.

"Where do they all stay?" Alice asked. She had been wondering if the overseas players were put up in a house or just stayed in hotels. They travelled around so much.

"He and Grant have got a flat in Bristol but they often crash at Graeme's place in Gloucester."

"Do you think he'll ask you to stay over with him? And will you, if he does?" Staying over would mean sleeping with him. Becky, like Alice, was still a virgin.

"He hasn't yet but he might. And yes, I think so." Becky blushed.

Alice realised she was going to end up the last of the three to lose her virginity at this rate. Jules had lost it ages ago and was probably sleeping with Leafy already.

She had fantasised a few times about Mr Walker taking her all the way in the pavilion. If he hadn't broken it off but had instead thrown her to the floor, ripped her clothes off, and had his way with her just as brutally as he had kissed her.

She had imagined him losing his resolve at the barbecue after stripping off his shirt, taking her in his arms, stripping off her own wet t-shirt and crushing her against his amazing body.

Alice wasn't sure which scenario she preferred. She liked the idea of a man taking control and getting so carried away that he just took her, overriding any doubts she might have. But she also liked the thought of something more mutually passionate, with the man showing concern for how she was and what she wanted.

Maybe the reality was totally different. Or maybe she could try both. It wasn't the kind of thing they were very clear about in the magazines or books she had read. They mainly talked about birth control and had a few diagrams of different positions. The only person she could really ask was Jules but she had hesitated so far. What if her fantasies were weird? She was pretty sure Becky's idea of sex was all honeymoon and rose petals and gentle embraces. Romantic rather than raunchy.

9. Euphoria

At sunset they were heading through the countryside on their way to a rave that Kate had told them about. "It's up on some sort of hill near Stroud," she had said.

Kate was driving them which worried Alice as she had no idea how they would get back if Kate got wasted. She supposed she could drive Kate's car for her.

It was easy enough to find as loads of other vehicles were heading there. This was a relief to Becky has she had worried that Brett and his mates, who were travelling separately, might get lost and not make it.

"The police will be here soon if they're not already," Kate said.

"Will they break it up?"

"I doubt it. They left Lechlade alone, it was too big to stop."

Sure enough they saw flashing blue lights as they approached and found that roadblocks were already being set up. "It's all off, it's over," a policeman told them, trying to wave them away.

"Bullshit," Kate said, though not to the officer. "They always say that to try and break it up. We'll just have to leave the car and walk the rest of the way." Kate managed to find a nearby field with an open gate and they parked in there, as other vehicles had done. Alice was glad they were all wearing Doc Martens, the mud from earlier rain would have wrecked most other shoes.

It was a steep climb up the hillside to Selsley Common. The sun had just gone down by the time they arrived and the sky was still light. You could see for miles across the Cotswold hills, rolling green fields divided by trees and hedgerows, villages strewn about, church steeples. It was like being on top of the world.

At the summit there were already thousands of people with the action taking place around a bowl-shaped dip. Sound systems, cards, vans and drink sellers surrounded the huge crowd dancing below them.

"That's going to be a mud bath by morning," Jules said.

Becky was fretting about meeting up with Brett. "I had no idea it would be so big, how are they going to find us?"

"How many of them are coming?" Jules asked.

"I don't know, Grant is but I'm not sure about the English players."

Kate had vanished to find her friends. She eventually reappeared with a dreadlocked bloke whom Alice assumed was Leafy. He wasn't too bad looking. His dreads were tied back off his face and he wore an eyebrow piercing and a baggy army surplus jacket.

Jules was trying to play it cool but was obviously thrilled to see him.

"Come over, we're having a smoke by Mush's van," he said. They went with him. Mush turned out to be another bloke with dreads who was completely out of things already. There were a couple of girls there as well. One had dreadlocks with her hair shaved underneath on the sides. The other had nose and lip rings and stripey tights covered with holes.

Alice's and Becky's DMs and jeans felt like school uniform by comparison. Jules was wearing her awful multicoloured baggy trousers again, similar to Kate and Leafy so at least she blended in.

Leafy sat down and started crumbling hash into a roll-up. He took a couple of drags and then passed it to Jules.

"Alice works at a vet," Kate said to Leafy.

For some reason this sparked interest. Mush came out of his daze. "You got anything on you?"

"What I am supposed to have?" Alice asked.

"Special K. Ketamine. All vets have it. You should have told her Jules, she could have brought some," Kate told her.

"Didn't think of it," Jules said.

Alice knew that Jules knew that not in a million years would she have taken substances from work. She was annoyed at Kate though.

"I don't want to stay here, I want to find Brett," Becky said to Alice in a whisper.

Alice didn't particularly want to sit around smoking either. The dance pit had more appeal. She needed something though. A drink would do.

A guy caught her eye. "Rhubarb and custard? Doves?" Alice had no idea what she should be asking for.

"Let's go and dance or something Becky," she said and steered Becky off to where the action was.

"I hate this music," Becky said. She was still stressing about Brett.

"They'll get here eventually, you can hear it for miles. Come on." She bought some drinks and they made their way down the side of the dip. She nearly slipped down, the grass was so muddy and wet.

You really needed something to get this music, Alice thought. She had planned not to take anything, but the night would drag with Jules off with Leafy and Becky hooked up with Brett, if he ever arrived.

A skinny lad with shaved hair was dancing around near them, flailing limbs, uncoordinated, lost in his own zone. When a light flashed over his eyes she saw his pupils like pinpricks.

"You want some pills?" he asked.

He only had one kind and judging by his eyes it wasn't what she wanted. She should have got Kate or Leafy to fix her up with something. Otherwise they'd just get ripped off.

They stayed and tried to dance for a while but Alice wasn't feeling it. She didn't really want to be here. It had seemed like a good idea at the time but now she wished she'd never agreed to come. She felt kind of bored and annoyed.

"Let's go back and find Jules. Maybe we'll find Brett if he's made it."

Becky was grateful for a change of scenery and they scrambled up the bank together. It was so steep that you had to take a run at it. There were people slipping and falling, struggling to make it.

Jules, Leafy and the other crusties were still hanging around the van but Kate had vanished. They were all increasingly out of it, but not as bad as Mush who seemed to have passed out altogether.

Leafy fixed Jules and Becky up and half an hour or so later as the rush was coming on Becky saw Brett and the others. She went from being the happiest person in the world to the happiest person in the universe and ran up hugging them all.

"We got lost around Stroud," one of them said. "Going round in circles, we had to stop at a garage to get directions. Then there were police everywhere."

Mr Walker was there. Alice was blissfully happy to see him but she was blissfully happy to see everyone and she just wanted to dance. She was energised and the music was suddenly much better.

Jules got Leafy to sort out Brett, Grant and another player that Alice recognised from the barbecue. Mr Walker and another dark-haired guy declined and went for drinks.

"Chris sent Stewie to keep us in line," Grant was saying to Alice. "But we all know why he's really here."

Alice was in love with the entire world, everything was beautiful. She hugged Grant then grabbed Becky who grabbed Brett and they headed back to the music leaving the others to follow. Alice could feel their joy. They were perfect.

It was a euphoric night. She lost all sense of time. They danced and danced for hours. Nothing mattered except the music and the night and all the amazing people around them. Alice was at one with the universe.

They were so high up on the hill, literally on top of the world. The lights of towns and villages were glittering like jewels.

Grant and one of the other guys had their arms around her and it was the best feeling in the world.

Then she found herself hugging Mr Walker. "I'm so glad you came. I was so hoping you'd be here."

Alice couldn't even remember how he responded. She was aware he wasn't happy like she was and she wanted him to be. "You are wonderful," she told him. She wrapped her arms around him and held onto him. She could feel every nerve in her body flowing into his. They were a single electric circuit. She could read his mind and it was more profound than anything she had known but she didn't know what it meant.

She was dancing again with someone, the entire hill was a dance floor. Everyone was one. It was unity.

Much of the night was a blur because time seemed to be really odd. She had only been dancing for ten minutes but then someone said it was an hour ago. She remembered the music stopping and someone who'd tried to rob people being chased by a crowd, and then it all started up again.

Then it must have been in the early hours they were sitting on the edge of the hill, maybe she was coming down, the sky was lightening at the edge. Some guy was massaging her shoulders and it was the most wonderful thing in the world. Everyone was happy. Mr Walker wasn't, he was nearby and he looked sad. Or was he angry?

"Why are you sad?" she asked him, trying to hug him again but he put her arms down from him. She picked up his hands and put them on her shoulders and for a moment he let them rest there and his very touch was like a golden light beaming through her flesh right into her soul, her skin felt orgasmic with joy, but then he took them off and walked away and she wasn't desolate because everything was still perfect, it was the most beautiful dawn in the world.

They all watched the sun come up. They being everyone, she thought, not just Jules and Becky and Brett and the others, but everyone there. You could see for miles, the sun was blinding. They had been given the entire world. It was theirs.

* * *

She was lying on grass. Damp grass. It was quite warm in the sun but she had no idea where she was for a moment. Then she realised she was outside Mush's van. Various other bodies were slumped down around her, and a few people were smoking perched on some plastic crates.

There was still music playing and people dancing but it all seemed thinner than she remembered.

Where was Becky? She could see Jules still passed out next to Leafy, if that heap of old army jacket was him.

God she was thirsty. And sore.

What time was it?

Everything was so flat. It was the most beautiful day, they were on top of the world, but it was a hollow world. An empty sky. He wasn't there.

Where was he?

"Do you need something?" It was Mush, he was offering her a wrap of something.

"No, it's ok." It wasn't what she needed. What she needed was gone. She had blown it. There was only one person in the world who could make the world less awful and he was gone. She buried her head in her hands.

"This'll help."

She looked at him. He was being kind but of all things there was school tomorrow, she just had to get through this. "Have you got any water?"

He handed her a bottle and she took a sip. She should be hungry, she thought, but she had no appetite. Jules wasn't even stirring. Alice was worried about Becky. Perhaps she'd gone back with all the boys. And Mr Walker. Or maybe she was still here?

She was certain he wasn't here. She felt now that she would always know, in her soul and in her skin, if he was near. She was wired to him now. Even if it was only one way, even if he had been sober and hadn't felt it. Even if all the warmth and the glow were gone now.

Maybe she had made an idiot of herself. But that was too much to contemplate right now. She closed her eyes again and lay back on the grass, the sun burning red through her eyelids. She could have covered them with her arm but she didn't. She wanted it to warm her brain.

Then they were back at Jules', God knows how Kate was in any fit state to drive but she got them back in one piece. No one had known where Becky was. But then there was a message left for them saying that she had gone back with Brett.

Alice wondered how she was. She hoped being with Brett would have eased the comedown.

"I always hate the day after but it was so worth it," Jules said.

"We probably should eat something healthy." Alice actually felt nauseous, but she thought this was probably more to do with low blood sugar. She was anxious about Mr Walker. Had she made a fool of herself?

"I feel like pizza or chips," Jules said. "Or a burger. But there's none of that here so it looks like toast."

They made a pile of toast with various jams and honey. The sugar did little to perk Alice up.

"You look miserable. Is that after effects or something else?" Jules asked.

"I think I blew it with Mr Walker."

"I doubt it. Grant said he was only there because of you."

"But I was all over him and he pushed me away. I think I embarrassed him," Alice said.

"He probably didn't want to take advantage," Jules said.

Alice wasn't sure what she should do any more. The ball seemed to be in his court, but left alone he might just find it easier to avoid her.

"You should confront him. Get him into the pavilion again and see if he'll have his wicked way with you."

It was a tempting thought but Alice didn't rate her chances of success.

10. Confrontation

He was blanking her again completely on Monday. Alice really didn't think she could take it any more. It was distracting her from her studies.

Not really caring if she made him even angrier she hung around until the end of cricket practice and went to speak to him. He was by the nets.

"Can I speak with you?"

Mr Walker looked around. There was only one other boy still left, clearing up some equipment. "OK, if it will only take a minute". He looked resigned. "You can go," he called to the boy who made a quick exit.

"Why are you ignoring me again?"

"Alice, we've been through this. There's nothing happening." He was trying to brush her off, busying himself with packing up cricket gear, not facing her.

"Why did you come to the rave then?"

"To keep an eye on the guys. Chris asked me to."

"They're grown men, they don't need babysitting. And why couldn't Chris do it?"

"He had a function." He looked up at her. The expression on his face showed finality.

Alice summoned her courage and looked directly back at him. "I know that's not why you came."

He said nothing for a few moments. She hoped he was wrestling with himself and that he would finally admit to it. But his better nature won out. "Alice, this isn't right. You know why. I work at your school. I'm old enough to be your father."

"Hardly." Not unless he was some kind of child bridegroom, he was at least twenty years younger than Richard. "My father is in his fifties." Her stepfather, but that was beside the point. Her real father would have been not far off also.

"I'm not discussing this any further. Just focus on your exams and forget about it."

She tried one final tactic.

"If I hadn't been at the same school, if I was just some girl you met in the Dog & Duck, would it be different? Would you be interested?"

He was silent and for a second she thought he wasn't going to answer her.

Then he said, his voice lower, "Maybe."

It was enough. One thing Alice had learnt from working at the vet - with animals and also with their owners - was that you had to be patient. They wouldn't trust you immediately, all at once. It took time, bit by bit, day by day. You built the trust. Just as she could wear Mr Walker down.

She was sure of it. She could have said something like "I know you want me" but it would have been too much. She needed him to think about it, let it linger in his mind.

So she left him, without saying anything more. She had won, and it might have seemed the slightest thing, but as an admission it was momentous. He did want her. He wanted her badly. At some point, his good resolutions would have to give way. She just had to be there when they did.

* * *

It didn't help that they got into a row with Maddy Pullen that week. Maybe it was the stress of exams, or just the time of change in their lives, but old rivalries seemed more bitter than ever. Or maybe Maddy saw her high school crown slipping into irrelevance as the year reached its end and wanted a final showdown.

It started in a Biology revision lesson which included both Becky and Alice. The teacher went out of the room to fetch something and for some reason an argument broke out. Afterwards Alice couldn't even remember what started it.

"You're such sad slags, hanging around with cricketers. Everyone knows what a groupie you are, Becky, you're giving yourself the worst reputation," Maddy said.

Alice couldn't sit back and leave Becky undefended. "At least she has a reputation, your name's just dirt everywhere."

Things devolved into a vicious slanging match ending with Becky and one of Maddy's friends having to physically pull the two of them apart.

The Biology teacher arrived back and sent both of them off to Mrs Paddington with a note.

Alice approached the Senior Mistress's door with dread in the pit of her stomach. She envied Maddy the fact that the she didn't even seem to care. She was just furious at Alice.

"Look what you've got us into now."

"You started it," Alice said. "You had no right slagging off Becky."

"She's just a stupid little slag."

Alice ignored her this time - if only she had managed to do so the first time - and they went in together after knocking.

"Why are you here, girls?" Mrs Paddington asked.

Alice handed her the note.

"Fighting? In the Upper Sixth, just weeks away from your exams? Surely one would hope for better behaviour than this. No, there's no excuse Madeleine, I don't care who started it or whether you're stressed over exams or not. It's unacceptable."

Not for nothing was the Senior Mistress called the Padlock. She gave them both a detention for the following afternoon which was Friday. This was pretty bitter as everyone liked to leave as early as possible at the end of the week.

"Better still you can report to Miss Symons for clean-up. Getting outdoors and some exercise will do both of you good."

Alice thought this was far worse. Regular detention just meant sitting back in a classroom and revising. With exams nigh, no one would make them waste their time writing lines.

Clean-up, which was a weekly sweep of the school grounds by those being disciplined for various offences, meant that everyone would see them. It was humiliating. Which was probably the point. At least Maddy, with more social prestige to lose, would hate it even more than Alice did.

* * *

Jules laughed her head off when she found out. "I'll bring a camera, this must be the last chance I'll get to photograph you in public disgrace. Pity it's too late for the yearbook."

"And the first actually, as it happens," Alice said. She had never been condemned to clean-up before. It was nearly always only juniors that got roped into it, making it all the more humiliating for them. Which was probably Mrs Paddington's aim.

Becky felt guilty and upset that Alice had ended up getting punished for her sake but Alice assured her it wasn't her fault. "I went off at her, I didn't need to."

"I'm glad you did," Jules said. "I've been wanting to slap her for over a year."

"How do you think she knew about Brett?" Becky asked. "I haven't seen her out anywhere."

"No idea. Maybe her sister saw us, she works in the Dog & Duck," Jules said.

"She wasn't there that night, I'm pretty sure I didn't see her."

"Maybe one of the other bar staff told her. If not that, then maybe someone saw us all at Selsley. I don't know."

Alice hoped it was the latter. If not, it meant Maddy might also have heard about her kissing Mr Walker. Maddy Pullen was absolutely the last person on earth she wanted to know about something like that.

Maddy's source would have to remain a mystery for now. Becky wasn't doing anything wrong dating Brett, and she was known as a sweet girl generally, so Alice wasn't too worried on her behalf. Getting involved with a staff member though was quite a different story.

It gave her more sympathy for Mr Walker's reluctance, not that she planned to let it go. She liked him too much for that and she was pretty sure, after confronting him this week, that he felt the same attraction.

"You seeing Leafy this weekend?" Becky asked Jules. Gloucestershire were playing away in Yorkshire so Becky wasn't seeing Brett. Which worked out well as she and Alice planned to spend the weekend revising for their Biology exam next week.

"Probably."

"What do you guys actually do? I mean is he always out of it?"

"No." Jules sounded defensive. "We just hang out and stuff. We talk about things."

"You're not planning to get dreads are you?"

"Maybe, when school's over. My hair's such a nightmare."

"I don't see why you need them. Kate doesn't have them," Becky said. This was beside the point since Kate's school wouldn't have allowed them either. "And I don't get how you can wash your hair if it's all matted."

"You use special shampoo. Or baking soda and vinegar."

"That's why they smell," Becky said.

Alice tried to change the subject as this couldn't end well. Privately she agreed with Becky but she didn't want to take sides.

"We should do something to celebrate next weekend," she said. "Surviving the first week of exams. I haven't got any the following week."

"I hate how they're all spread out and then clumped. It's like they don't give any consideration to what would make best sense in terms of revision. Why put both Economics ones in the same week?" Jules said.

"Still, once you've done Economics it's all over," Becky said.

It was amazing to think this was now only four weeks away. The end of school forever. Alice still got a sick feeling in her stomach when she thought about the approaching exams. The days were flying by far too fast.

"So what about you and Mr Walker?" Becky asked. Alice had told them about her conversation with him on Monday. They were all convinced something would happen eventually.

"Nothing more yet."

"You know he's divorced?" Becky said. Alice hadn't known. "I don't think Brett knows many details, just that he was married and they split up a couple of years ago. Maybe that's why he's so careful."

Alice hadn't known and it unsettled her. She was immediately obsessed with knowing what his ex-wife was like.

"She's his ex. So he obviously didn't want to be with her, or he would be, wouldn't he? Plus she's millions of miles away in Australia," Jules said.

"You don't know that. And she might have been the one to end it." It was going to torment her. "Did they have kids?"

"No, I don't think so."

"My stepmum's still on really good terms with Kate's dad. But there's nothing more there any more. She said they married too young and ended up like brother and sister. Maybe it's like that?" Jules said.

The thought of Mr Walker having a childhood sweetheart was even worse to Alice but she didn't say anything. Now she was going to be stuck brooding about it all week. And she couldn't go out and drown it out because they all had to behave that weekend. There was too much at stake.

11. Detention

Maddy was already arguing with Miss Symons when Alice arrived by the playing fields to join the rest of the group condemned to clean up. As well as Maddy there were half a dozen or so younger pupils there.

"I'm absolutely not wearing that. It's broad daylight." Maddy could be as stubborn as a mule when she wished. Alice was actually surprised she'd shown up at all.

The bone of contention was an orange reflective band which they were meant to wear for safety. Most people assumed, probably quite rightly, that its purpose was actually for humiliation.

"Madeleine, you will wear the band. It's required."

"My punishment is coming here and cleaning up. We have rights you know. You can't just deliberately embarrass us, even prisoners don't get that."

Miss Symons was getting increasingly exasperated and didn't want Maddy giving the younger pupils ideas. She turned her attention to Alice.

"You're late, Alice. I need you all to hurry up and get your collection bags. I won't be able to supervise you today, I have a meeting that's just come up. Mr Walker has kindly agreed to take my place."

Suddenly detention was simultaneously the most awful and the most amazing thing in the world.

Alice saw him approach, and from his face she could tell that he had no idea she would be there. He must realise that there was no way she could have known either.

"Thanks for helping out at such short notice, Stewart." Miss Symons hurried off, forgetting about the orange bands.

Alice felt odd and slightly resentful to hear her call him Stewart. I'm more familiar with him than you are, she thought.

"Are you supposed to be wearing these?" he asked them when Miss Symons had gone.

"No, they're just for the juniors," she lied.

Taking charge, he divided the juniors into two groups and sent Maddy off with the first to one side of the grounds. She scowled but obeyed.

Then instead of making Alice go with the second group he sent them off in the other direction without her.

This left the two of them walking alone with just Alice's collection bag as chaperone. Alice was both pleased and surprised. Her patience, she felt, was paying off.

"What are you in trouble for?" he asked.

"A disagreement in Biology. I think we're all a bit stressed about exams."

"Just a disagreement?" He raised his eyebrows. God, she loved being with him, even in these circumstances. He was so magnetic. When he looked at her she was mesmerised.

"A bit of a fight. Some stuff was said and I should have ignored it but I didn't."

He was concerned. "About you?"

"No, about Becky and Brett. Really it was nothing." She wanted to change the subject because it didn't present her in a very good light even if she had been defending Becky. "Are you enjoying it over here? England, I mean."

"It's not too bad. It has its attractions." His eyes lingered on her for a moment. Was he flirting with her? He really seemed to blow hot and cold.

"What will you do when term ends?"

"There's some coaching work at Gloucestershire, mainly for the youth squads."

So he would be here over the summer. She rejoiced.

"And you're off to be a vet?" he asked her. Alice didn't remember telling him that, someone else must have done so. She hoped this was the case since that meant he must have been asking questions about her.

"Only if I get the grades. And not immediately, Jules and I are going travelling first for a year. In Asia and Australia." She looked at him on this last word, and he looked back at her.

"What made you want to become a vet?"

Here's where you were expected to trot out the "always loved animals" line but Alice didn't, because that wasn't the entire reason why. "I thought it would be interesting, having so many different kinds of animals to study and work with," she said. "And also be something that you could travel and work overseas with. There are vet jobs all over the world and the qualification here is recognised pretty much everywhere."

"You won't miss your home town?"

"Do you?" she asked him.

"Sometimes. I like being on tour and working overseas but home is home."

"What's it like, Sydney?"

"Just like the photographs show. Great beaches, lots of national parks. Loads to do whether you're a tourist or a local. Definitely worth a visit," he said, looking at her again.

She got the message. He wanted her to come. He actually wanted to see her again in the future, even though it might be months away. Was that what he was waiting for, for her to finish school? If he could just say so it would help.

"There's no way we'd travel as far as Australia and not go there. Unless we run out of money or something." She smiled at him. She saw that it disarmed him.

They continued to walk along the side of the cricket pitch. Alice picked up a few pieces of litter if she saw anything, there wasn't much, and Mr Walker did too even though he wasn't supposed to. Whether he was unaware of that or whether he just wanted to help her out she didn't know.

But she was glad as it stopped it feeling like a punishment, they were just two people picking up litter. A team. She finally felt that he was acknowledging that they were on more familiar terms than everyone else.

"What was it like playing cricket? Did you always want to do it?"

"Was it my boyhood dream do you mean? Not initially. That was to be a train driver." He saw her eyes widen. "When I was about seven, anyway. After that I wanted to be a top business executive, wear sharp suits like my Uncle Rex and have an office at the top of my own tower. Then when I was about fourteen or fifteen I realised I could make a go of the cricket, or my coach did, and that seemed more appealing than numbers."

"You're glad you chose that? No regrets?" She hoped it wasn't a stupid question.

"None at all. I still read Economics at university, thinking it might come in useful if I changed my mind. Or this happened." He indicated his shoulder where the injury was. "So it still might. It's healing well but you can't keep playing forever."

"W G Grace played well into his sixties." Alice couldn't remember how she knew this. Possibly Jules had told or there had been something about it at school once.

Mr Walker laughed. "He was a local boy wasn't he? Times are a bit different now."

Alice didn't think W G Grace, with his enormous Victorian beard, could fairly be described as a "boy" but she took his point.

"I'm doing Economics A-level. It's the last of them."

"For veterinary science?"

"You only need two sciences. I couldn't face Physics, and I thought it might be a back up option if I didn't get into a veterinary degree. I could do business studies or something," she explained.

"Much like me then. I hope you get your first dream though."

They were approaching the pavilion now and all she could think of was the time he had kissed her in there. He had been so angry. She wondered if he was thinking about it as well.

He had fallen silent. Alice took a risk.

"Do we need to clear up inside the pavilion?" She knew full well it was an outdoor clean up only.

She saw him wavering. A muscle clenched in his jaw.

"Do you think we have something to clear up?" he asked her.

"I think that could be the case."

She was so nervous she was amazed she could speak. He was only just hovering over the edge. At any time he might change his mind, step back.

But he didn't. He opened the door and ushered her in before him. Inside the light was dim as the shutters were drawn.

He stood before her, still on the brink but increasingly resigned.

"What do you want from me, Alice?"

The answer was so easy. She reached up around his neck and his arms went around her and his lips were on hers. Their mouths opened, his tongue intertwined with hers. It was sweet, sensuous.

She smelled his scent, she had grown to crave it. His skin, the faint soap or aftershave he used, the cotton of his shirt.

Her hands felt the nape of his neck, the shape of it, how it tapered to his collar. His hair was cropped so short she could feel the gradient from hair to skin.

"You," she said as he buried his face in her neck and her hair, breathing her in as well. "I want you."

"God, Alice…" she loved how he said her name, his accent, the rasp in his voice that betrayed his desire for her. His need. He's fighting it, she thought, but he needs this as much as I do.

They knew they couldn't stay in there for long, it would look suspicious if anyone saw them. Maddy might already be suspicious over Alice going off with him in the first place. She could always make something up about him wanting to talk about Becky and Brett or something. She started inventing a possible conversation in her head.

He was telling her again how wrong it was.

"I lack all self-control around you. It's not a normal thing for me. I've usually got a better grip of myself. This really has to stop. I'd get sacked and it would be terrible for you. And you know I'm too old for you."

He was rejecting her once again.

"Let's get back and we'll just forget about this."

Two steps forward, one step back. She would have to be patient again. At least he wasn't angry any more.

* * *

Back at home Alice didn't bother telling her mother or Richard about the clean-up. She didn't want to worry them. She figured if a note was sent home she would deal with it as and when that happened. Most likely it wouldn't be, it would get overlooked amid everything else that was going on this term.

"I'll cook tonight," she said, feeling she should make some kind of amends to the universe.

"Don't worry about that. The Baystons have asked us over for a last minute supper. It's ok if you need to revise though," her mother told her.

Alice was on the fence about going. She was revising all weekend anyway and could afford a couple of hours. The Baystons, old family friends, were nice people and she liked their dog. They also had a cat which was due to have kittens any day. On the other hand it would be glorious to get the house to herself for a while.

She was still flipping a mental coin when Richard arrived back from work.

"Has the Baystons' cat had her kittens yet?" Alice asked.

"A few days ago I believe. Four, Sheila said."

That decided it. Four bundles of mewing fur would be preferable to brooding at home as she knew there was only one thing - one person - who would occupy her mind. Even though she saw plenty of kittens at the veterinary practice Alice never got tired of them.

"Do we have to dress up?" she asked her mother.

"No, just casual."

Alice went to get ready. She wondered what Mr Walker was doing that evening. She hoped he'd be sitting around at home kicking himself for rejecting her once again.

* * *

Dominic Bayston opened the door to them. Alice wasn't expecting him to be there. He was a year older than her and was already at university. He must be home for the weekend. Years ago she had had a crush on him but it went unrequited and they were just friends now.

As expected her younger brothers went into raptures over the new kittens and Alice had to restrain them from stressing the tiny animals out by diverting their attention with a box of Dominic's old Lego.

"Poor old Whisky isn't getting much love," Dominic said, referring to the ageing beagle. Alice rubbed its tummy.

Dominic had an elder sister who was several years older than him and worked with horses in Ireland. She had got married a year ago. The Baystons were overjoyed to share the news that she was pregnant with their first grandchild.

Baby talk didn't interest Alice or Dominic so they went into the games room after supper. Alice's family couldn't stay late because her brothers had to be put to bed, but the adults would probably chat for another half hour or so.

"How are A-levels going?" he asked.

"First ones are next week. I just can't wait until they're over and we get the longest summer holiday ever."

"And Fairmount, still okay?" Dominic had gone to a different school but she had known him since childhood.

"Same as ever. How's Manchester?"

"It's not so bad. Full on." He was reading engineering in the north of England. "You still planning to be a vet then?"

"Yes, or I'll find out in August anyway when the results come out," Alice said. There was something else she wanted to ask him.

"You remember that girl at your school, Sally something? Had to leave because she got caught with a music teacher. What happened to them?"

"She moved in with him when she went to sixth form college, then it fizzled out after she went to university. He followed her up there and it was all a bit pathetic from what I heard," Dominic said.

It hadn't wrecked her life then, Alice thought. The local newspaper had got hold of the story at the time and it had been a town scandal. Particularly as the music teacher had been married and had left his wife for the girl.

Dominic was stroking the new-mother cat. It looked large, sleek and exhausted. "I only came down to see Bessie's brood but don't tell my parents. They like to think I'm homesick."

"They are sweet. Will you keep one?"

"I'd love to but it wouldn't really work in a flat. Mum's got them all promised to various women in her ladies' group. The kids move out, they get a cat."

Alice thought of all the unwanted kittens they ended up with at the veterinary practice and wondered if there was a way to link supply with this demand.

"How's your friend?" Dominic asked.

He meant Becky not Jules because he used to have a thing for her.

"She's good. Still planning to do physio. She's going out with an Australian cricketer who's playing for Gloucestershire." Alice thought she had better mention it in case Dominic had wanted to give her a call.

"Nice for her." He didn't sound resentful, he must have moved on.

"Do you think you'll come back here, once you graduate? Do you think most people will?" Alice asked him.

"Not with what I'm doing, there won't be the jobs here," Dominic said. "But others might. I wouldn't mind staying up in Manchester, it's pretty great. Lots on and cheaper than London."

That was the thing about everyone going away to universities in other towns and cities. It broke ties. Alice couldn't imagine not being near her family but she also struggled to imagine herself running a local practice like Jo. She knew she wanted to travel. She would face a choice some day.

PART II

Boundaries

Into such a sudden zest
Of summertime joys

Epithalamion, Gerard Manley Hopkins

12. Revision

Alice went over to Becky's house on Saturday morning to start their revision session. Gloucestershire were still away playing in Yorkshire so Becky couldn't see Brett anyway. Alice was surprised how quickly their relationship had cemented. It seemed like they had been going out for months, not just a few weeks.

They were in Becky's parents' kitchen as there was a large table by the window they could spread all their notes out on. Alice was finding it hard to focus on cell division and membranes and transport.

"I don't think they'll ask us about this," Becky was saying about a particular topic, "because apparently they did last year. It was in our mocks if you remember. They always change it every year."

Alice thought back to a few years ago when she couldn't have imagined in a million years choosing Biology. When she was younger she had dreamed of working in an ice cream factory, then being a florist, and at one point being an air hostess. Her parents had tolerated all these fantasies knowing that eventually, like pretty much everyone else at Fairmount, she would be steered into a traditional and conventional profession.

"Do you remember when we first did this back in Junior School?" she asked Becky.

It had been far more simplified then and had disappointed them all, as they had assumed that "Asexual Reproduction" must be something to do with sex. Discovering it was all about amoeba had been an enormous let-down. An even worse disappointment lay in store with the next chapter in their "Biology 11-13" textbook, titled "Sexual Reproduction". This turned out to be about flowers.

It wasn't until the following year that their class had finally reached the long-awaited, highly anticipated section on Human Reproduction. Of course by then they knew everything about it anyway, or thought they did.

Alice remembered the staid biology teacher hurriedly reading through the entire chapter in a dry monotone, pausing once or twice to ask "any questions?" and then immediately resuming before anyone had the chance to put their hand up. If he wanted to bore them off ever having sex he had made a good effort.

"It was with Mr Coleman, wasn't it? It was awful. I vowed that day I was never going to have sex ever, because it sounded so dull and mechanical and I couldn't get his voice out of my mind," Becky said.

"I imagine Brett's relieved you didn't keep that resolution," Alice said. Becky hadn't directly revealed whether she and Brett had gone all the way yet, but Alice assumed they must have done.

"He was actually surprised I'd waited this long."

"What was it like?" Alice asked.

"Honestly? The first couple of times it was pretty awful. I hated it the first time but I didn't tell him. It just hurt so much and I hadn't a clue what I was doing," Becky said.

"Do you think he realised?"

"I hope not."

"So it got better?"

"Yes, definitely. It's great now. And I'm glad I got it out of the way," Becky told her.

This surprised Alice. Out of the three of them Becky had been the one most leaning towards waiting for marriage and doing the whole Cinderella thing.

"I think there's a danger of waiting too long," Becky said. "Rach told me about this girl on her nursing course who broke up with so many boyfriends because she wanted to wait, and then she got married and it was awful. It never got better. Turned out the only reason he'd been happy to wait was because he wasn't really into it." Rachel was Becky's elder sister.

"It could be even worse. You might find out they were into something weird," Alice said. She remembered her mother once letting slip about a divorced friend whose latest partner wanted her to do something unspeakable on a glass coffee table while he lay underneath and watched.

"But the main reason is I think you can end up investing too much into it," Becky said. "I always thought I wanted to wait, and then I met Brett and it didn't seem like so big of a deal any more. It was just something I hadn't done yet, not this massive thing that was sitting in the way."

Alice agreed. She wished she had got it out of the way with the boy she had dated for a few months the previous year.

"Would you do it with Mr Walker if he wanted to?" Becky asked.

God yes. "I think so, probably."

"I'd be scared about doing it with someone like him. I mean he must be so experienced, mustn't he? He must have slept with so many other women," Becky said.

Miserably, Alice imagined a string of glamorous and sophisticated women knowledgeable in the most exotic sexual arts lining up outside his bedroom. How could she possibly compete?

They put their noses back to the grindstone for a while but Alice's mind kept wandering.

As she was trying to force herself to concentrate on single celled organisms, Becky's mother came back from her shift at the hospital. She greeted them and asked how the revision was going.

"It's ok," Becky said. "We'll never be completely ready. How are you?"

"Rather tired but I promised your Aunty Brenda I'd go bowling with her." Aunty Brenda wasn't Becky's real aunt, just a family friend.

"Before you go I nearly forgot, can we lend Jules that old tent in the garage? The one Andrew used for school trips. I'm sure he doesn't need it at the moment," Becky said.

"Of course you can. Is she planning a camping holiday?"

"Something like that." Jules wanted it to go to a festival with Leafy. She hadn't wanted to turn up with a brand new tent. She was finding it quite an effort to make it appear that she wasn't making an effort.

Becky's mother put the kettle on and took out some biscuits and put them on a plate. At Alice's or Jules' house they would just eat straight from the packet. Becky's family did everything in a more proper fashion.

Alice thought about all Mr Walker's doubtless skinny model-like exes and wavered over the biscuits. "You need your energy," Becky's mother encouraged her. "All these late nights revising. Keep your strength up." She also put out some fruit for them, grapes and some cut up apple. Alice took a slice.

"It's got serious pretty quickly, Jules and Leafy," Alice said when Becky's mother had gone.

"I know she really likes him but I don't know about his side. He always seems drunk or stoned whenever I've seen him. I sort of wonder if he's as much into her. Don't say anything to her though."

Alice felt bad for hoping that Becky was right. She wanted the old Jules back. She didn't want to travel round Asia with Jules washing her hair with vinegar and being permanently stoned. That was of course if she even came.

"I also forgot to ask you about the clean-up," Becky said. "Was Maddy a total bitch? Did she even show up?"

"She was there. But that wasn't the biggest surprise." Alice told Becky about Miss Symons leaving and handing over to Mr Walker.

"No! Did he ignore you again?"

"Actually the opposite. We had the first decent conversation in ages. It was nice."

Becky looked at Alice. "And?"

"And we kind of ended up in the pavilion again. Only for a moment though," she said, seeing Becky's mouth fall open.

"Did he kiss you?"

"Yes. Or I kissed him. I started it really." What do you want from me, Alice? he had asked her. And he had known full well. Because he wanted the same. If only they had had more time, if only he had fewer scruples.

Becky was still agape. "Jules was right. I honestly thought that he wouldn't go there again but I didn't want to upset you. I really thought he was going to hold off. But Jules said he'd cave eventually."

"I didn't know either way. I'm glad though. Even though it was back to square one again right afterwards with the usual I'm-too-old stuff," Alice said.

"Maybe that's why Jules was so against this at the start. Because she could see how into you he was, that it wasn't just bit of a drunken snog. I mean particularly with what's happened since. He's really hooked on you. Otherwise he would have just cut you dead the first time and that would be that."

Alice had no idea how Jules would have known what Mr Walker's intentions were after one evening in the Dog & Duck as she hadn't even known herself.

"I wonder what would happen if school found out. Do you think they really would expel you?" Becky asked.

Alice imagined being hauled before Mrs Paddington and asked to explain her "improper relations" with a member of staff. Or would they consider she had been taken advantage of, and be all sympathy?

"They'd still have to let me sit my exams. When that guy a couple of years above got kicked out for drugs just before A-levels they let him back." The boy had had to sit his exams in a separate room with another teacher invigilating. He also hadn't been allowed to wear school uniform.

"I'm not sure why they regard it as a privilege to wear school uniform. I'd much rather sit my exams in jeans," Becky said. "Not if everyone was staring though."

It would be weird never having to wear uniform ever again. School uniform anyway. Both of them would have a kind of uniform given the careers they had chosen. Alice thought of Jo in her white veterinary coat.

"I heard some of the boys are going to burn their blazers on the pitch on the last day."

"We should join them and throw our gym knickers on," Alice said.

Images of a bonfire and the symbolic destruction of Fairmount Class of 92 flared before her eyes.

"Imagine if someone actually held a rave on school grounds. If a load of travellers and ravers showed up and took over the cricket pitch."

"All the vans in a ring around the wicket. Spiral Tribe in the pavilion."

"Everyone getting high and waving glowsticks at the Padlock."

"Imagine."

13. At the cricket

It was Wednesday, the eve of their first Biology exam, followed by Chemistry on Friday. Alice had already taken the afternoon off work so she could do any last minute revision she needed to. She and Becky had been revising non stop since the weekend. Teachers always warned against last minute cramming but it always worked for Alice. Today, though, she was crammed to the hilt.

"Why don't you come to the cricket?" Becky asked her. "They're playing against Worcestershire in Gloucester."

Sitting watching county cricket wasn't Alice's idea of high excitement but it was a beautiful day and it would be relaxing. Plus she could take some notes with her.

"Jules is going to drive us. Leafy and the crew have headed down Bristol way for some festival so she's going to come and bring her dad's pass. Brett said he could probably get us into the members' enclosure though," Becky said to further encourage her.

"I'll come. I'll bring some revision with me if that won't look too antisocial."

"Great. We're skipping lunch so we can get there earlier." It hardly mattered any more, so what if they got into trouble? What was the worst that could happen to them, the day before their final exams started?

It was something Alice was finding unexpected about that last school term. She had expected it to be like any other term: full on classes and schoolwork right up until the exams started, then the exams, then some kind of ending.

But it wasn't turning out that way at all. The whole term had been different from the start, as though even the teachers were disconnecting from them. It was just revision and a sense of being on your own at last.

The exams were all at different times, and some people's last exam took place weeks before others finished. And you were free to go once they were all over. There wouldn't even be a final day when they would all walk out together, throw all their notes in the bin, shred their school ties. Instead they would leave in batches, the summer holiday starting with a trickle rather than a bang.

Alice remembered the year above her, how faces had gradually drifted away. You didn't think about it until afterwards, but that was that. Now they were the ones who wouldn't return. There wouldn't be a next term. There wouldn't be any more school, ever again.

Jules had been to the cricket ground before so knew the way, helping them arrive in good time. It was the second day and Gloucestershire were batting. Alice recognised several of the team. She could just about follow the scoring but even the players didn't seem very engaged with the game.

It was pleasant sitting there nonetheless. Very English, Alice thought. The green of the field and the white of the players' clothing and the gentle pace of the game. The knock of leather on willow as Jules' father would say.

The Worcestershire deep fielders seemed to spend most of their time giving the eye to them and any other girls in range rather than watching the ball. If the three of them had been single it might have been fun. Alice supposed she was single but her interest lay firmly elsewhere.

Mr Walker wasn't here of course, as there were school matches on.

A tall and good looking dark haired player had been giving Alice particular notice, causing Becky and Jules to keep nudging her.

"Cut it out, we're not in the fourth form," she said to them. A month ago she would have been thrilled with his attentions, admittedly.

She looked after their seats when they went off to get some drinks. Alice saw Chris by the pavilion, and he recognised her and came over for a few minutes.

"Enjoying the action?"

Alice wasn't quite sure if he was joking. The play looked soporific to her.

"Yes, it's nice weather for it." She felt self-consciously English as she said this. The Australians had joked about their national obsession with the weather.

"Stewie not with you?"

She started. "No, he's back at school."

"Schoolboy cricket. Of course." Chris grinned, watching the play. "Not quite what he's used to. You both coming out this weekend?"

Alice was again surprised by the question. "I don't know, I mean I suppose so if he's out with you and Brett and everyone and we all meet up somewhere."

Chris gave her a glance, taking his eyes off the field for a moment. "Hasn't he asked you out yet?"

Her stomach flipped. Was he supposed to? "Not really. More the opposite."

Chris raised his eyebrows then looked back at the game. "It's hard for him you know. He really likes you but he's cautious." Alice was practically dissolving inside at this.

"He's been deliberately keeping his distance," she said. Since last Friday he had avoided any contact with her and she had felt devastated all over again. But now with what Chris was saying the world had literally flipped around for her once more. Chris was talking to her as though he thought she and Mr Walker were a couple. She needed to set him straight.

"It's not easy for him," Chris was saying. "The divorce was hard on him, he's been wary ever since. And you're a lot younger than him. The boys having a go hasn't helped."

She loved that despite all this, Chris still seemed to assume that it could all happen. "What was she like, his ex?"

"Bree? A sort, you know. Better off with the footballer she ditched him for. More glitz and getting her photo in the papers."

"How long has it been?" She felt guilty for asking, like she was snooping on him. After all he'd never even told her he was divorced. She knew practically nothing of his past.

"Two, three years now. Don't worry, he's long over it." He spoke to her like an equal which reminded her of Richard.

She wanted to ask what Mr Walker had actually said to Chris about her but thought it would make her sound girlish and needy.

"I'd better get back. Have him bring you up on the weekend, we're playing Somerset."

The week after was clear of exams so the weekend was open. She'd have to talk to Becky and figure something out. Despite what Chris seemed to think she wasn't in a position to discuss weekend plans with Mr Walker. The fact that she still thought of him as Mr Walker pretty much said it all, though she avoided calling him by any particular name to Chris.

Becky and Jules arrived back. "Chris have anything to say?" Jules asked.

"It was kind of awkward. He spoke about me and Mr Walker like he thought we were a couple."

"You're both crazy about each other. It's pretty obvious," Jules said. Once again Alice felt herself surge inside.

"But nothing's happening. He keeps pushing me away," Alice said.

"Except for the constant trysts in the pavilion. And he came to Selsley don't forget. It was obvious why he came."

It appeared to be obvious to everyone except Alice. "He didn't lay a finger on me though. Absolutely nothing happened that night."

"You were sky high. I expect he didn't want to take advantage."

Alice felt exasperated. "So what I am supposed to do?"

"Just wait until he's a bit drunk again," Becky suggested. "There's a party in Gloucester on Saturday night. I'm sure Chris will drag him along."

As the game continued the good-looking fielder continued to give her the eye whenever he was positioned near them. "You going to be in the bar afterwards?" he asked when the ball was the other side of the pitch.

Alice knew she should really head home and revise. Maybe an hour or so wouldn't kill her so long as she didn't drink anything.

"What do you reckon Becky?" She'd let Becky decide.

Becky was obviously keen to see Brett and Jules didn't have an exam the next day so was up for it.

"Maybe," she told the cricketer. He looked slightly familiar. Perhaps she'd seen him in a bar.

He grinned at her and returned his focus to the game.

"He is really fit," Jules said. "You should go for it."

"I'm just not interested."

"Well I would be. If it wasn't for Leafy obviously." The fact that Jules admitted this gave Alice her first ray of hope since the whole Leafy and crusties thing had begun. Old Jules was still in there somewhere.

"I told Brett we'd have to leave early because of Biology tomorrow. Do you think it will look too keen if we all go and hang out in the bar now?" Becky was fretting.

"I think you're past that stage now," Jules said. "It's not like you have to tiptoe around any more. You are his girlfriend now, officially."

Becky looked embarrassed but happy. "OK then."

They sat back to watch the final play. The dark-haired cricketer had been moved to a different location and since there was no one directly near them on the boundary, Alice got out her notes and did a bit more revision. She'd read it all a thousand times but you never knew. Maybe some critical fact or formula would stick in her mind just that much bit more with repeat readings.

* * *

They were the centre of attention in the bar after the match. The dark-haired cricketer zoned straight in on them bringing others with him including Graeme.

"You're only on mineral water?" he asked Alice. "Driving?"

"Exam tomorrow."

"School or university? Where do you go?"

"School." If they were out on the pull they usually lied and said college but all the Gloucestershire players knew their ages because of Brett and Becky. "In Cheltenham."

"Really? That's where I'm from, I went to school there too. Fairmount," he said.

"Same. You must have left a while ago, I don't remember you."

"My little brother's still there, doing his A-levels too."

The penny dropped for Jules. "You're Joe Jackson aren't you? Can't believe I didn't realise earlier. I heard you played for Worcestershire."

He smiled showing white, even teeth. "Big cricket fan then?"

"No, my dad is. But everyone's heard about you because of Mike. Plus your name's up on a plaque of glorious old boys."

Joe got a ribbing from the other players for this but laughed it off.

"Are you all coming to this party on Saturday night?" Graeme asked. It was at someone's house in Gloucester and everyone seemed to be going. It was a Bank Holiday weekend.

"Hopefully," Alice said.

"Look forward to seeing you there then," Joe told her.

"You still going to be around?" Jules asked, thinking that the Worcester team would have moved on by then.

"We're playing in Birmingham, so not far." It was about an hour's drive down the motorway from Gloucester.

"You missed a huge night in Stroud the other week," Jules told Graeme.

"So I heard. And that your Headmaster was there too." He looked slyly at Alice when he said this.

"Mr Francis?" Joe asked, surprised. Fairmount still had the same Headmaster as in his day.

"Not their actual Headmaster. A mate of Chris's who's coaching at the school. Has a thing for Alice." Joe raised his eyebrows at this.

Alice wanted to sink through the floor, even more so when the man in question entered the bar the exact same moment.

"And here he is. Your round, Stewie?"

She dreaded to think how she looked to him, sitting at the bar surrounded by a load of guys. She looked at him but his expression was impassive, he gave her no signal whatsoever.

Jules was biting her lip trying not to laugh.

"You're coaching my brother?" Joe asked him. "Mike Jackson?"

"Yes, he's a good kid. Got some talent," Mr Walker said.

"Don't tell him that, he's as cocky enough as it is." Joe was sitting there with his arm on the bar in such a way that it was half around Alice. She saw Mr Walker notice this, briefly flick his eyes to hers and then look away. Her heart sank.

She didn't know if Joe was deliberately trying to play up and annoy him, but he leaned slightly closer to Alice and even brushed her arm when he reached for a drink. He also made a point of getting her a new drink. Alice felt incredibly uncomfortable and hemmed in. She also felt guilty even though it wasn't her fault.

Joe also brought up various reminiscences and anecdotes of former events and teachers at Fairmount, deliberately trying to establish a rapport with Alice and cut Mr Walker out. Joe was completely focused on her and it was hard for her not to respond without seeming rude.

Alice wasn't sure if he liked the challenge, was trying to score against the more experienced man, or was acting out of some misguided rescue instinct.

She had always imagined that having two men contend over you would be hugely flattering, particularly when they were both so attractive. The reality was just awkward and embarrassing. She felt annoyed with Joe and bad for Mr Walker, and she was panicked that he might think that she was encouraging it.

He completely ignored her, not saying a single word to her. She couldn't even try to include him in the conversation because he eventually sat apart from their group drinking with Chris.

It was a relief to finally leave.

"That was a bit of a chest baring," Jules said as they drove back afterwards.

"What do you mean?" Becky had been oblivious, wrapped up in Brett as usual.

"Joe Jackson putting the moves on Alice deliberately to rile you-know-who. I wonder if there'll be a fight on Saturday?"

"I'm sure Mr Walker's not going to the party." Alice said.

Jules laughed. "Of course he will. They're all going. And more importantly, you're going to be there."

"They won't really fight will they?" Becky asked.

"I hope so," Jules said. "And that someone gets it on camera."

14. Party

With the first exams done and dusted and no more for nearly another two weeks, they were ready for fun. The party that night was being thrown by one of the players in Gloucester. "It's practically a mansion," Becky had told them.

"They don't have mansions in Gloucester, it's a hole," Jules said. She had been persuaded to come as Leafy was somewhere else roaming around the countryside in a convoy. The festival they had been heading to in Avon was cancelled and everyone had been driven away by the police.

Now they were all looking for somewhere else to go. There were news reports every night about travellers' vehicles getting turned away all over the country. Mush, Leafy and their crew were currently stuck somewhere in a lay-by near Stroud.

"Let's get dressed up tonight," Becky said. If they all glammed up it would be ok. Just one of them in a little dress if the others wore jeans would look odd.

Alice was tempted to go shopping for a new outfit but she also wanted to save her money for her trip. Particularly as her veterinary job was on hold until exams were over.

Becky being petite could get away with anything and had loads of great clothes passed down from her sister as well as her own wardrobe. She was spoilt for choice and willing to lend but everything was too small a size for the others. Jules and Alice could just about swap clothes though Jules was taller.

"Is this too nightclub?" Becky asked about a white frock she was trying on.

The problem with parties in summer was that they started ages before the sun went down. Nightclubs were easy, they never went until around pub closing time when it was long after dark. Alice didn't want to look too sweet or too slutty. If Mr Walker was there - and in her heart of hearts she knew he would be - she wanted to make the right impression. He had only ever seen her in school uniform or jeans. And her tennis skirt, she remembered in embarrassment.

"White is more day, but it's shiny-ish so you're fine," Jules said.

Alice picked something short, black and backless. From the front it looked relatively demure. From the back it was anything but. If it turned out to be over the top she could just stand with her back to a wall.

"You can practically see your arse in that dress. I presume it's for lover-boy's benefit?" Jules herself was wearing something tight and purple she'd bought from Top Shop ages ago and the others had to beg her not to pair it with Doc Martens. Instead she was forced into a pair of Becky's sister's old heels that were half a size too small.

"You do look amazing Alice," Becky said. "Like a popstar or something."

Alice tried to protest out of embarrassment but even Jules agreed. "You are way more attractive than Maddy or any of those girls. They only get all the boys because of who they are at school. Plus everyone knows Maddy's easy. But a guy like Joe Jackson isn't going to be all over just anyone like he was over you the other day."

What Jules said about Maddy was true. If you weren't in the top echelon of cool at school you simply didn't date anyone else there. The premier clique dated one another, everyone else looked on. Alice's former boyfriend had been from a different school.

"Won't it be great to be past all that?" she said. "I can't imagine anyone cares about that stuff at university." There would still be different social sets that formed but at least they'd get to start from scratch.

Because the party was too far for a taxi and they didn't want the mortification of a parental lift, Alice offered to drive. It meant staying sober unless they all ended up crashing somewhere, but that had its benefits. If she'd made an idiot of herself in front of him when she was high at least she wouldn't do so again.

"Graeme still likes you," Becky said to Jules. "He's always asking about you."

"Just because Leafy's not here it doesn't mean I'm going to get off with someone else."

* * *

Happily the party was already in full swing by the time they arrived. It wasn't exactly what Alice would consider a mansion but it was a pretty large house. She wondered who owned it and how trashed it would be by the next day.

Becky immediately went off with Brett when she found him and Alice and Jules ended up talking with a group of Somerset players.

"Are there any good clubs around here?" one of them asked.

"Rockefellas, if you like hairdressers and flinty looking fifteen year olds from Gloucester High," Jules said.

Alice was on edge wondering if Mr Walker was here already and if not when he would come, and if he would come at all.

Her dress was causing a bit of sensation. Some of the guys viewed it as an open invitation to grope her back. She might have found it funny if she'd had a few to drink and she wasn't stressing about Mr Walker seeing her with a load of men again.

Rescue came in the form of Joe Jackson, who swooped in and put a protective arm around her.

"Hands off."

"Is this your girlfriend?" The Somerset players were apologetic.

"She goes to my little brother's school. I'm her bodyguard for the night." He planned to be more than that though, Alice thought, judging by where his hand was.

Joe was caressing the base of her spine - no one could see, thank god - and she was trying to not like it. His fingers were trailing a really sensitive spot and making her skin shiver. Feeling guilty, she tried to arch her back and break the contact.

He laughed and put his arm further round her body, grasping her hip. This was worse. It actually looked like she was with him.

At any other time of her life she would have been over the moon about this. A guy a bit older than her, really good looking, a successful sportsman. But she wanted something different now, someone else.

They were plied with drinks on all sides and it was a struggle to stick to soft drinks. She kept telling people she was driving but the drunker they got the less they remembered or the less they cared.

Jules rolled her eyes. "Just have one Alice and we'll figure out another way home. Your car will be ok here overnight."

Alice supposed Jules was right so accepted the next drink offered. Beer was pretty much the only option available.

"Going to finally get you drunk, am I?" Joe was really trying to put the hard word on her.

Of course it would be exactly at that moment that she saw Mr Walker. He was wearing a light blue shirt that matched his eyes and he looked amazing having been out in the sun all day. He had the kind of skin that went gold rather than sunburnt.

She tried to squirm away from Joe once again but it only made it worse as he grabbed her to him, thinking she was messing around. Mr Walker saw everything.

Jules was no help because Graeme had made a beeline for her and was chatting her up in the corner.

"It's the Coach!" Joe said. "Is he still after you, Alice?" He called him over but Mr Walker just nodded and left the room. Alice was desolate.

"I have to find the bathroom." She slipped out of Joe's grasp and headed in the direction that Mr Walker had gone.

Finally able to approach him she had absolutely no idea what to say. "Hi. I wasn't sure if you'd be here."

He looked down at her. Even with her wearing heels he was far taller than her.

"Did you come with Chris?" she asked.

"I think you should get back to your boyfriend, Alice." He was firmly in school coach mode or trying to be.

"He's not my boyfriend."

"He seemed to appreciate your dress." He let that one slip, she thought, and felt a tiny surge of joy.

"We only met the other day. I know his brother." It's not how it looks, she wanted to say, but that was such a cliché. She wished Mr Walker would run his hand down her back. It was pretty much the only reason she had worn the dress.

Maybe if she just went to kiss him he would yield? Something held her back though, given there were so many other people around. It wasn't that she minded them seeing but she didn't want to embarrass and annoy him.

"Can we go and talk somewhere?" she asked.

"That's not a good idea. You know why," he said before she could protest.

Just then Chris came up. Alice had never been more relieved to see him. Maybe he could fix this and make it happen.

"Managed to find your girl, Stewie?" he said.

Alice felt radiantly happy at the acknowledgement.

"Alice was just going back to her friends." It was a command, not an observation.

She wanted to defy him but he was clearly resolved to keep her at arms' length. Yet again. She couldn't hang around the two men with one of them barely refusing to speak to her. He had won this round but she was determined that she would win the next.

Perhaps she should go all out and flirt back with Joe and the other guys to try and provoke an even stronger reaction in him?

What held her back was the guilty knowledge that she would quite enjoy flirting with Joe but it would seem a betrayal. Then she felt annoyed. After all, she was a free agent. Mr Walker was constantly pushing her away. Maybe she should just go and have fun, to hell with it.

She managed to find a bathroom on her way back and bumped into Jules there.

"Did you find him?" Jules said.

"He blew me off again. Made some snarky comments about Joe Jackson."

"He's jealous! That's great."

"Not if he gets too jealous though. He might just give up."

"If I were you," Jules said, "I would just go for it with Joe Jackson. He's clearly up for it. You know he's being tipped for selection to the England squad?"

This didn't mean a great deal to Alice as she didn't follow cricket. All the same she had to fill the evening somehow.

When she returned to the room where Joe was she found him already surrounded by another group of girls. Before she could make an exit again he saw her. "You're back." He pushed past the other girls and put his arm around her. So it was settled, she thought. She was effectively his date for the night.

He was young, he was handsome, he had bright blue eyes and tousled dark hair that he pushed back off his forehead. He ticked every box. But he wasn't Mr Walker.

Still, he was obviously a bit of a player, so she didn't feel too bad about leading him on.

* * *

They ended up outside in the garden: Joe, Alice, Graeme, Jules and a couple of others. The evening was balmy and there was a half moon in the sky. Despite the skyglow from Gloucester the stars were also bright.

As Becky had said, Graeme was still clearly keen on Jules. If Jules got drunk enough she might just yield, Leafy or no Leafy, Alice thought.

Someone passed a joint around and the familiar tang filtered through the night air. Alice skipped it because it wasn't her thing and she wanted to keep some wits about her.

She had tried to get drunk but it didn't seem to make her feel any better. She envied Jules who was in high spirits, telling various outrageous stories. Alice felt she was sobering up more quickly than she could drink.

Joe didn't seem to notice she was quieter. He had his arm around her shoulders and his other hand was resting on her thigh.

Maybe Becky was right. Maybe she should just lose her virginity, get it over and done with. Joe might be ideal for the job.

Thinking about this she went to the bathroom again. All the alcohol was going straight through her. She kept an eye out for Becky and of course Mr Walker but didn't see either of them.

"Have you seen Matt anywhere?" some girl asked her. Alice didn't recognise her and she hadn't heard of anyone called Matt.

It was one of those parties that got busier the later the hour as people were continuing to arrive after the pubs shut. The downstairs cloakroom was occupied so she made her way up the stairs to find another. A house this large must have several.

There were still people upstairs - couples mainly - but it was less crowded than downstairs. Various bedrooms had been taken over and there were empty glasses strewn all up the stairs and on the landing. Whoever owned the house had a massive clean up ahead of them.

Alice found an unoccupied bathroom and locked the door. After going she sat on the edge of the bath for a while, her thoughts confused. What was she doing? Where would this lead?

Eventually she got up and looked in the mirror. She was still looking ok. She swivelled to try and see where her dress was positioned and hitched it upwards and forwards a bit to avoid her underwear showing.

As she exited the bathroom she bumped into one of the Somerset players they'd spoken to earlier. "Jackson not with you?" he asked.

"He's outside," Alice said and instantly regretted it because the guy was leering drunkenly at her.

"Come and have a drink with me."

"No thanks, I've got to get going," she said. The drunken player was pawing at her, not letting her past him to the stairs.

Afterwards she couldn't remember exactly how it happened. He had somehow manhandled her through a bedroom door and pushed her onto the bed. She was crying out but he put a hand over her mouth and pushed her dress up.

He was swearing at her but his words were slurred. Alice thought she heard "fucking cocktease" but her ears were ringing with panic and everything was a blur.

He used his bodyweight to pin her down. He had a heavy, chunky build and he stank of booze and cigarettes. It made her feel sick. She couldn't move.

"Let me go," she was pleading with him, but he was groping her roughly, forcing his fingers beneath her underwear, trying to rip it off.

She was crying in fear but no matter how she struggled she couldn't get away from him.

Where was everyone else? Why did no one come?

His hand was over her mouth again, practically covering her nose, she could hardly breathe. She couldn't even bite his hand because he was mashing her lips against her face.

She was getting exhausted from struggling against him, trying to escape.

His body squashed hers and with his other hand he was fumbling with his own zip. He'd got it stuck and he was swearing again and calling her names as he got angrier.

If he had been only slightly less drunk he might have been less clumsy and things could have been a lot worse.

The rest of the events were almost like being in a trance.

There were voices and shouts and suddenly he was pulled off her and she was lying there dishevelled, trembling and weeping. Her dress was in disarray, perhaps torn.

Two men fighting and a punch and one dragging the other out of the room.

Someone was asking her if she was alright, some girl, and Alice was huddled into a ball. The girl had her arm round her, trying to console her.

Finally, the only people she wanted to be with were there, Jules and Becky. Joe was also there but Alice was barely aware of him as her friends took her into the bathroom and closed the door. They were both hugging her as she sobbed.

"He's scratched your face," Becky said and dabbed the blood off with a damp tissue.

She never knew how long they stayed with her but eventually she was ok again and they helped her fix her dress and walked her down the stairs, one on either side of her like bodyguards.

Joe was very concerned about her and offered to drive her home.

"You're way over the limit," Jules said.

"She should go to the hospital," Becky said.

Alice managed to say that it hadn't gone that far, that she was ok, just bruised and shaken up.

"You could still press charges though."

But she just wanted to be home, in her own house, in her own bed. She wanted to take a shower and wash every trace and memory of his horrible clammy hands off her, his raw beery breath.

In the end Joe ordered them a taxi. He wanted to come back with them but they assured him they would look after her. "You can go and beat the living hell out the arsehole who did this," Jules told him.

"That's already been taken care of. Not by me, worse luck, or he'd be the one needing hospital." The player had been dragged off somewhere while they were looking after Alice and no one was quite sure what had happened to him. Or who he was.

"Did you recognise him?" Becky asked Joe.

"No. We're due to play them next week. He's in for a bat round his skull if he so much as shows his face."

They bundled Alice into the taxi, getting in after her, and gave the driver her address.

"I really am fine now, you guys can stay on at the party."

"No way are we leaving you," Jules said and the three of them travelled together back to Cheltenham.

Alice was so glad of them. So grateful. No one in the world had such amazing friends as she did. They didn't ask her anything about it, didn't make her relive it. They were just there for her.

Alice's parents were asleep when they got back at around two o'clock in the morning, so they tried to be as quiet as possible.

"I'll run you a bath, you can soak it all off," Becky said.

Getting out of the bath Alice was overcome with a wave of exhaustion so intense that she could barely pull a t-shirt on.

She had feared that when she tried to sleep she would be kept awake by visions of his leering face and her terror and panic. But when she closed her eyes there was only gentle darkness.

15. Aftermath

They all slept in until nearly midday on Sunday. Alice's mother didn't disturb them but when they eventually wandered down the kitchen she looked concerned. All the more so when she saw the scratch on Alice's face and that her lip was bruised.

"You've had several phone calls, Alice, all from men asking how you are. What on earth has happened?"

"Some guy got a bit too drunk and had to be thrown out of the party," Alice said.

"But look at you! What happened to you?"

Alice really didn't want to say. It would only worry her mother and she felt totally fine now. It all seemed to have happened a very long time ago.

"This player got a bit friendly with Alice and had to be pulled away," Jules said. She guessed that Alice wanted to play it down to her family.

"It was all very quick and nothing really happened," Alice said, seeing her mother's alarm. To try and change the subject she asked who had rung.

"Someone called Joe rang and left his number," Alice's mother said, looking at the notepad by the phone. "Then there was a Graeme. And someone who sounded Australian who didn't leave a name or number."

They all caught one another's eyes. No prizes for guessing who that was.

"Will you call Joe?" Becky asked. "He was pretty great last night, getting us the taxi and everything."

Alice really didn't want to call anyone except the one number she didn't have.

"I'll call Graeme," Jules offered. "They must have broken for lunch by now and if he rang at eleven o'clock he probably gave the dressing room number." She went into the hall to use the phone and was gone for a short time while Becky and Alice rather nervously chewed toast. They couldn't really discuss things in front of Alice's mother.

Eventually Jules came back and it was clear from her face that she had something she needed to tell them. "Graeme was just checking how you were, he'll let the others know you're ok. It's caused a bit of a stir because apparently that arsehole has done this before and was already on his yellow card. So now he's out."

"You mean from the team?" Alice asked.

"Yes. I don't think he was their star player, I'd never heard of him and you know how my dad goes on about cricket all the time."

"We should get outside, it's a lovely day," Becky said. Like Alice she was dying to know what more Jules had to tell them.

"Should I ring Joe first?" Alice asked. She didn't want to be rude.

"You can do that later. Worcestershire are playing in Birmingham today aren't they? I'm pretty sure that's not a Birmingham number as my aunt lives there and her code is different. So it's probably his home number from Worcester or wherever he lives."

It was a beautiful late May day and very sunny. They didn't have school tomorrow thanks to the Bank Holiday and no one felt like revising. Jules suggested they went down to the beer gardens in town and sat in the park there. "We can get some crisps and stuff and try and get a tan."

* * *

The beer gardens, more formally known as the Imperial Gardens, lay between the Town Hall and the town's grandest hotel. Being such a central location they attracted large crowds on a sunny day and there was a good chance of bumping into people you knew.

They bought some snacks from the nearby off-licence and found a spare stretch of grass next to a flowerbed of garish, regimentally-planted petunias.

"Civic flowers. They're always really fake looking, aren't they?" Jules said.

"We want to know what Graeme said." Becky and Alice were getting impatient because Jules had refused to reveal anything until they got there.

"Do a little drumroll for me then," Jules said.

"Come on!"

Jules finally yielded. "Someone we know may be walking around with grazed knuckles today." This left them none the wiser. "Your rescuer, Alice, the one who ripped that Somerset arsehole off you and punched his lights out was none other than your beloved Mr Walker."

Alice didn't know how she felt. Glad and grateful, of course, and thrilled, but also anxious.

"I never got a chance to thank him. I never saw him again that night, not since way earlier," she said.

"He was there the whole time, just brooding and avoiding you I imagine. You were pretty full on with Joe." Alice felt ashamed at this.

"But you can't blame yourself," Jules continued, seeing her face. "Mr Walker took himself out of the running. Anyway he was there all along, and by coincidence or whatever he saw you being assaulted and saved the day."

"Where was he when we left?" Becky said.

"No idea. Probably outside giving the guy a good thrashing. We were in the bathroom for some time. He may have left the party then, but I doubt it. You'd think he would have wanted to speak to Alice, check she was ok. Especially since he rang the next morning."

Alice felt even more terrible for having had Joe around while they were leaving. "I just assumed it was anyone at the party. I had no idea it was him," she said.

"Now he's your rescuer. So you'll have to find some way to reward him." Jules grinned, and then her own face fell as she looked over at another group of people. "Oh god, of all the people who could be here today, it's Maddy Pullen."

"Where?"

"Over there, with the usual crowd of them. I hope they don't see us."

But Jules hoped in vain. Maddy saw them, then held some kind of conversation with her friends while giving jeering glances, and then came over.

"Not shagging any cricketers today? Finally get dumped for someone better, Becky?"

They knew better than to rise to her bait.

"How did you find Biology?" Alice asked, referring to the previous week's A-level exam. She had noticed Maddy looking particularly stressed and miserable when she came out of the examination hall.

Maddy scowled. "It was fine and I don't need to get an A in biology anyway."

"You don't even need any GCSEs to do what you're doing," Jules said.

"Actually you need ABB to do Sociology," Maddy told her.

"I wasn't talking about Sociology. I was referring to your degree in being a stupid slag."

"Look in the mirror if you want to see a slag," Maddy said. She turned to Alice. "And what were you up to sucking up to Mr Walker last Friday, going into the pavilion with him?"

Alice felt her heart thump. She must not, must not give anything away. "He wanted some litter picked up in there."

"Very cosy I'm sure. Just as cosy as your night in the Dog & Duck?"

"I have no idea what you're talking about."

"Just some very interesting rumours that I heard, but I couldn't possibly believe given you're such a sad ugly cow. Now I wonder," Maddy said.

"You can wonder all you want," Jules told her. "The only nasty rumours around here with any truth in them are those that feature you."

"Yeah, well there's no way he'd lower himself to you lot anyway." Maddy left, not satisfied that she'd scored any direct hits.

When she had gone the others were silent until they could see she had rejoined her group and was well out of earshot. Alice felt physically exhausted. With the events at the party last night, and what Jules had just told them about her rescuer, Maddy hearing something about Mr Walker and her was all too much.

"She knows. What am I going to do?"

"She doesn't know anything. She's just digging," Jules said.

Becky, who had been lying on her side, sat up. "She doesn't want to believe what she heard because she likes him herself. I heard her talking about him in class. You've got nothing to worry about."

Alice disagreed but didn't want to dwell on the subject. She thought it was far more likely that Maddy would stir out of jealousy, if what Becky said was true.

"Whatever happens it's only a few more weeks now. Then we're free of it all. No more Maddy ever." Jules was trying to reassure Alice, but all Alice could think of was no more Mr Walker, ever. She figured the link via Becky and Brett would still be there, but there wouldn't be the daily opportunity to see him. It was a miserable thought.

"Will you ring Joe tonight?" Becky asked.

Alice supposed she would have to. She was grateful to him but she really didn't want to lead him on any more. Now he had taken on the role of her protector he possibly had expectations and she would have to let him down. "I guess so. I'm not sure what I'll say though," she said.

"Don't stress it. He's not going to be devastated if you turn him down. I'm sure he has other girls lining up around the block. He certainly will if he gets an England cap," Jules said.

"What about Mr Walker, will you call him too?"

"He didn't leave his number," Alice reminded Becky.

"But what about school next week?"

"I'm not sure, if doesn't go out of his way to avoid me I'll try and thank him," Alice said.

Just then Jules gave an excited wave. "Kate and Tash are here!"

Tash turned out to be the non-dreadlocked girl from the Selsley rave. There was also another guy with them whom they introduced as Jez. He was small and nondescript save for his t-shirt printed with an elaborate sun design.

126

"We're going up to Castlemorton later. It's absolutely huge, there's thousands of people there," Kate told them.

The Castlemorton festival, described as an illegal rave by the newspapers, had been making headlines the past couple of days. Tens of thousands of travellers and ravers had congregated on common land in the Malvern Hills in Worcestershire, driven away from an earlier, cancelled festival. Police had been powerless to turn back so many people and it was anarchy.

"What about school?" Jules asked.

"It's a Bank Holiday tomorrow, remember? And this is the gathering of a lifetime, it's massive."

"Bigger than Lechlade?"

"Way bigger. It's like a supermarket for drugs. All the sound systems are there," Tash said.

"We've got space for you in the car if you want to come," Kate offered.

Jules had an exam the next week and was hesitating. Becky didn't want to go since Brett wouldn't be there. Alice didn't care either way.

"Leafy's there," Kate said. Jules knew this but the nudge was enough to help her decide.

"OK, let's go. We'll have to pick up some stuff first. What time are you planning to head up?"

"Whenever. It'll be light for hours. Late afternoon, early evening maybe?" Kate said.

"It'll be better when it's dark. Easier to avoid any police on the way." Tash pointed out.

Alice was starting to feel excitement. It was such a last minute thing to do, go all the way to Worcestershire, she liked the impulsiveness. She would have to lie to her mother and Richard because they had been tut-tutting at the television news reports every night and would freak out if they thought she was planning to go there herself.

* * *

Back home Alice threw some things into a bag and waited for Jules to call her. Her parents were watching the news again and there was more coverage of Castlemorton. Their sympathies lay with the nearby villagers who were sick of the disruption, rather than the party goers. Alice felt a guilty twinge about her plans. Not enough to change her mind though, the scenes of revelry on the television only acted as a greater drawcard.

The phone rang, it was Jules. "Bad news. Kate's car is kaput and I can't borrow either of my parents' ones, not overnight anyway. The others have managed to get a lift with someone else but there's no room for us."

Alice was dismayed. "There must be some way to get there?" They discussed different options. It was in the middle of nowhere so even if they got a train to Worcester it wouldn't be much use. There wouldn't be any buses at that time of night and taxis probably wouldn't want to go near the area due to the police. Alice's parents both needed their cars the next day.

"We could try and hitch a ride from Worcester or something?" Jules suggested. "There must be other people heading that way. They're arriving all the time according to the news."

"It's nearer Malvern isn't it? Is that on the train line?" Alice asked.

"Not sure. Anyway Kate's making a few calls, the problem is all her mates are already up there."

"Call me back if she has any good news, otherwise let's give it half an hour and just get a train and hope for the best."

Alice replaced the handset. Immediately it rang again. "That was quick," she said.

"Is that Alice?" A male, Australian voice. Definitely not Jules.

Oh god, it was him. Mr Walker.

"Sorry I thought you were Jules," she said, confused.

"I was ringing to find out how you were after last night."

She knew from that moment, from the tone of his voice, that the battle was won.

"I'm fine, thank you so much for your help. I didn't realise it was you who intervened until today."

There was a short silence. Then he spoke. "I was wondering if you'd like to meet me for a drink tonight?"

Her heart leapt. But she couldn't let Jules down. "I would love to, but Jules and I are going to the Castlemorton festival." Please let him suggest another time, she thought.

"The one on the TV?"

"Yes. Our lift fell through so Jules was trying to arrange something else. That's why I thought you were her when you called," Alice said.

"I'll drive you both there."

She was stunned. "Seriously, you don't have to do that. It's miles."

"It's no problem. Besides I'd be interested to see it for myself. It looked like quite an event on the news."

This was unprecedented. She was trying to get her head around it.

"If you're absolutely sure, I'll call Jules. Her sister needs a lift too, will that be ok?"

He said it would be and asked for her address. "I'll pick you up in half an hour. You can direct me to Jules' place.

Alice sat on the chair in the hall for a while, still in shock. Then she remembered she had better phone Jules. The number was engaged the first two times she dialled but eventually she got through to Kate. "Oh hi Alice, I was still trying to sort us out some transport. No joy yet."

"It's all sorted. Put Jules on."

Alice told Jules the developments and Jules started laughing. "My god. We're going to an illegal rave with a teacher. This is the most insane thing ever." She rang off, leaving Alice wondering how she was going to explain Mr Walker's arrival to her parents. She decided it would be best to just wait outside and get in his car before they saw.

16. Castlemorton

Mr Walker arrived exactly when he said he would and got out and opened the door for her. For the first time Alice found herself feeling horribly shy around him. She was still fearful that he might think she was fickle for being around Joe all night.

"He scratched your face," he said.

"It's nothing, it's barely anything." She felt more embarrassed about the whole episode than traumatised now.

"I wish I'd got to the bastard earlier."

Alice got into the front seat, and looked across at his profile as he pulled into the road. He also seemed to be avoiding looking directly at her. Maybe he was still hesitating, still wavering? She sensed that he was torn between wanting to be with her and what he thought was doing the right thing. It would be interesting to see how he would act at the festival.

They drove to Jules' house and Jules and Kate got in the back. Jules was all sly grins to Alice, who hoped that Mr Walker couldn't see. She knew that any pointed remarks or innuendos from Jules would only send him further away again.

Instead they talked about the festivals and the whole movement, Kate leading the conversation as she had been involved in it for so much longer.

"Is there anything like in Australia?" Jules asked him.

"In the outback they have B&S balls - bachelor and spinster - that get pretty wild. But they're organised parties," he told her.

"What about travellers?" Kate asked.

"Not so much. Bikie gangs are more of a thing. Then carnies, but they only travel with fairgrounds."

"Yeah, they're not the same," Kate said. "So you work at Jules' school?"

"Something like that."

"Nice, giving us a lift. Can't imagine any of my teachers offering."

Alice felt excruciating embarrassment. She wished Jules had tipped Kate off about the situation with Mr Walker beforehand. Or perhaps she had and Kate was being clueless or deliberately stirring.

She glanced at him as he drove. His eyes were fixed on the road, if Kate's words had unsettled him his expression gave nothing away.

Alice also wasn't entirely sure what his intentions were with the festival. He had said he was interested in seeing it, but did he plan to stay there with them or just drop them off, take a look around and leave? She wasn't worried about how they might get back, there would be any amount of people heading back at the end of the holiday weekend who they could get a lift with.

* * *

None of them had been to Castlemorton before so Alice had to map read. As they got nearer to the Common it was obvious because there were cars everywhere, parked all over the place. They found their own spot and got out.

The throb of music could be heard in the distance, and there were people still arriving, making their way towards it.

Tash had described it as a "supermarket for drugs" but it was a supermarket for everything rave related. There were stalls selling bottles of water and cans of beer, glowsticks, whistles, music tapes and various drug paraphernalia. An entire shanty town for partying.

"It's vast," Jules said. Among the many smaller tents there were several large marquees, each a party in itself. Different sound systems were playing, the music blending and clashing as you walked between them. Caravans, cars and lorries everywhere, all different colours.

On the way to find Mush's van they passed several encampments of travellers. They had campfires, dogs and small children running around. Alice wondered what they must think of all the noise and ravers. For a fleeting moment she imagined Jules and Leafy like this, living on a campsite somewhere, raising a family. She could see the appeal of the freedom, the alternative life, the travel. But she still hoped it wasn't what Jules would end up doing.

"It's so beautiful here," she said. It was beautiful. The sun was setting on a day of glorious weather, the sky was a vast dome over rolling green fields and hedgerows. The colour and noise of the people and the music, the scattered tents and vehicles, formed a vibrant carnival. Even without taking anything it was beautiful.

"How will you know where to find your friends in all this?" Mr Walker asked. The festival stretched for what must have been nearly a mile.

"They'll be here somewhere, we always find one another." Alice wasn't sure how Kate could be so certain, but sure enough they came across Mush's van with the usual motley crowd hanging beside it.

"You made it," Tash said. Jez was standing nearby, dancing by himself. A spliff was passed around.

Mush had got a bottle of vitamin pills and was drawing smiley faces on them, selling them to unwitting ravers for a fiver each. He was making a killing.

"It's doing them a favour really," Tash said. "They're not buying anything dodgy and at least they won't OD. Most of them are already high."

Alice thought it was deceitful but she couldn't argue with Tash's logic. She remembered when a boy at Fairmount had sold fake acid tabs to several girls. They had convinced themselves they were tripping and made idiots of themselves. They never lived it down.

Leafy offered to fix them up with something real but Alice declined. For several reasons she had decided not to do anything that night. Except maybe a beer. She wanted Mr Walker to see her sober, not off her face.

She realised that everyone was coupled up - if you could count Mush and Kate as a pair - with Jules happily reunited with Leafy. That left her and Mr Walker, who wasn't taking anything either. He didn't look very comfortable in the gathering.

"Let's go for a walk and find some beers," she suggested and he went with her.

If this was a date, it was the strangest date ever. Perhaps if she got him drunk enough again it would be easier. She hadn't even thought about how they would get back, or when.

They bought several cans - he paid, though Alice tried to - and then looked for somewhere to drink them. There were people going up and down a fairly steep hill that flanked the festival area. "Do you want to go up there? There must be a good view from the top," he said.

Alice wanted to be on top of the hill with him more than anywhere else in the world. It was a harder climb than she expected but eventually they were on the summit. And the view was spectacular.

In the growing dusk the colours of the festival were fading but it was starting to glow with light. They drank the beers in silence. There really wasn't anything to say. Alice felt a deep gladness that she had come. This festival was something else. She would remember it for a lifetime. She would remember being on this hill, with him, with the sight of it stretching out before and beneath them.

She really wanted him to put his arm around her, to kiss her, but he didn't touch her at all. He just sat there, drinking a beer. She wanted to taste it on his lips so badly.

There was a helicopter flying overhead.

"Police?" he asked.

"They can't break it up because it's too big," she said. But she wondered if the scene could continue. The parties were getting bigger, wilder. This one was making headlines all over the country. Something about that night, the mood, her own life with school finishing soon, it all felt like the end of an era.

"How long will it last?"

Alice wasn't sure. "Until it fizzles out or they bring in the army."

A couple of beers later she was feeling more spirited again. She wanted to dance or at least be nearer the music. "Let's go back down."

Once again he came with her, half running down the steep slope because it seemed easier to get down it quickly than slowly.

They found Spiral Tribe, one of the sound systems, near the centre of it all. It was open-air unlike some of the other systems which were in large marquees. An assorted collection of vehicles formed a circle and people were dancing inside it.

Round the fringes there were frequent offers of pills, mushrooms and other substances. A girl was shouting "Acid! Ketamine! E!" at the top of her voice. Alice turned them all down.

"You're not taking anything this time?" he asked.

"I don't always. I mean I hardly do ever really." She was loosened up enough by the beer that the music sounded better, but it didn't have that amazing, all consuming quality it did after taking ecstasy. "Do you ever?"

"Not for years, since university."

Alice had no idea where the others were. She could only vaguely remember the direction of Mush's van. She wanted to dance but she felt awkward asking him, and she couldn't just start dancing in front of him.

Then miraculously she saw Jules, lost in the music. She grabbed her and Jules flung her arms around Alice, hugging her and saying all the usual things that Jules said when she was as high as a kite.

"If you want to wait here I'll get some more beers," he said.

"Don't get lost. Remember the spiral," Alice told him. The sound system had a huge black and white spiral symbol hanging from the side of one of its vans.

Even though she wasn't high she was soon fuelled with adrenalin just from being there, the night, the music, Jules being crazy happy, all the people.

Mr Walker came back and they drank more beer, and even though he showed no signs of wanting to dance it didn't matter. Everything there was a spectacle. Some guy who had allegedly been mugging people was chased and pinned down by a group of ravers. Flares were fired at police helicopters. People milled all around, dancing, walking, drinking, wasted.

They moved from place to place, visiting the areas where different types of music were playing. They bought food. The ground was strewn with rubbish.

Then the others had gone for a bathroom break and Alice was alone for a moment, just outside one of the marquees. A short distance away she saw a group of ravers standing around something - a girl - slumped on the ground having some kind of fit. The people with her were all absolutely wasted and were staring like fish.

Alice wasn't so drunk that she couldn't recognise the girl was in serious trouble. She went over. The girl was on her back and vomiting, coughing and choking. Some instinct took over and Alice rolled her over, tried to clear the vomit from around the girl's mouth.

"What did she take?" she tried asking the people watching but they were useless, absolutely off their heads.

Then the girl convulsed and was suddenly still. She was unconscious. Alice moved her over but she was limp. Had she stopped breathing? Her chest seemed still. She put her ear to the girl's mouth and felt nothing. No warmth, no breath. They had done first aid at school but the rubbery Resusci-Annie dummy was nothing like this.

Alice pulled vomit out of the girl's mouth with her finger. Hoping she had the head in the right position she tried breathing into the girl. She was terrified. Her hands were shaking and she was trying to find a pulse. Was it young people or old people whose wrists didn't work? She could never manage to find the carotid artery. She grasped the girl's wrist and nearly wept with relief when she felt a pulse. She gave her another breath.

"Get help!" she yelled at the crowd, there were more people gathering but Alice barely noticed them.

Afterwards she wasn't really sure whether everything had moved very slowly or lightning fast. She remembered the terror, the feeling of helplessness and frustration because everyone seemed too out of it to do anything. She remembered keeping up the rescue breathing, checking the pulse, but for how long she wasn't sure.

Suddenly there were paramedics. They were taking the girl from her, lifting her onto a stretcher. "Do you know what she took?" one of them asked but Alice shook her head. She could barely speak.

"I don't even know her, I just found her." She felt dizzy, she could taste the girl's vomit in her own mouth.

"How long has she been like this?"

Alice didn't know. She couldn't even guess.

They left with the girl and she was standing there, unsure what to do. She turned round and Mr Walker was there. She sank against him and clung to him. She was weeping and she didn't know why. His arms were around her and he was telling her that it was ok. "Let's get out of here," he said and she didn't argue.

17. Release

She could barely remember the drive home. She just knew she was exhausted, wasted, shattered. The image of the girl was there every time she closed her eyes. And with it all those stupid, drugged up idiots dancing around, not realising or caring that someone was probably dying. Was the girl dead? Would she ever find out?

Alice didn't even realise until he pulled up in an unfamiliar street that he hadn't taken her home. "Where are we?" she asked.

"I didn't think your parents would appreciate seeing you like that. Come back to mine and have a shower and some coffee first."

He had taken her to his place. Even if he claimed to only have altruistic intentions it was still crossing a line.

Alice was too zoned out to even look around her. She let him usher her up the stairs and to the bathroom.

"There are clean towels in there," he told her.

She let the shower take her over, wash everything away. She sank to her knees and cried with the water, cleansing the night and the smoke and the beer and the mud. Drowning the images in her mind in the constant fall of hot, wet drops. She didn't know how long she was there. It could have been minutes, it felt like hours.

Finally she left the warm cocoon of steam and wrapped herself up in a towel. It was large and white.

In the mirror she saw her face, bare of make up, her hair slicked back and wet. She felt returned to something, a new state, a blank slate.

Coming out of the bathroom and not really knowing or thinking where she should go, she walked into the room across the corridor. It was the bedroom. He was in there, he had just taken off his shirt.

He was disconcerted. "I'm sorry, I didn't hear you come out."

She couldn't speak.

Then he was silent too, and looked at her, his grey-blue eyes directly gazing into hers.

She felt fragile. He looked so powerful, the breadth of his chest, the strength of his arms. She ached for him.

And then he was there. Before her.

He put a hand on either side of her head, tilted it towards his, and brought his mouth onto hers. It was firm yet gentle. Nothing like the violent kiss in the pavilion. This was tender, exploring. His tongue probing her, drawing her own tongue into his mouth. They interlocked, soft and wet, quenching a thirst.

The towel slipped from her and she was naked before him. She didn't feel embarrassed. She saw the desire in his eyes and it made her feel desirable, that she had nothing to hide from him.

He moved his hands to her shoulders as she reached up to him, and Alice felt his hands slide down her back, warm and dry, making her skin tingle. He brought his hands around her sides and brushed his thumb over the side of her breasts.

She shivered and arched up to him. Then his mouth was on her neck, open, firmer. She felt him drawing her in, sucking on her skin. It would mark her again, but she was glad of it. She wanted to be marked as his, to have a sign that proved how much he wanted her.

Then she felt his lips move down her neck, across her chest. His hand cupped her breast and he brought his mouth down upon it. Her nipple swelled taut as he swirled his tongue over it.

Then his other hand was between her thighs. She knew where he was going and she trembled in anticipation.

They remained wordless. It was skin on skin, body pressed against body, a shared need. He had suppressed this for so long and she had longed for it for so long.

She felt his fingers slide between her legs, finding her slick and wet, wanting him like she had never wanted anyone before. He probed her entrance and she flinched at the sensation then gasped as his thumb rubbed over her clitoris. No one had touched her like this, so gently yet masterfully.

Then he picked her up and carried her to the bed, laying her down. He knelt over her and began kissing her again. His shoulders were so huge and strong. She put her hands against his chest, feeling the flat, hard planes and the heat of his skin. She reached around his back, clinging to him, wanting to run her hands lower to touch other parts of his body but not quite daring.

Now his head was lowered to her breast again, the soft skin of her stomach caressed by his left hand as his right cupped her breast and took it in his mouth.

Alice had a sudden flash of all that had gone before: the Dog & Duck, school, the pavilion, his reluctance. She thought of him coaching cricket and being a member of staff, an authority figure, his resolve to keep a proper distance from her finally eroded by desire.

She cried out as his head went between her legs and his tongue slid between her folds. It was as though he knew her body better than she did. He teased her opening with the tip of his tongue before moving up over her nub with more pressure. It was like a white light was concentrated there, the strained strings of a violin, tension, an electric sensitivity. Images came into her mind and she writhed against him as his fingers gently probed where his tongue had just been, firmer, harder, just a little deeper.

He brought her to the edge but wouldn't take her over it. Instead, just as she thought the wave would come over her he broke off and moved his body back over hers. He pressed the length of his torso against her, skin against skin, crushing her with his weight. It was deliberate. He was showing her his strength, his power, his need.

She doubted if he would even let her get away now. He wanted her so much that it was beyond rational thought, just pure, physical need to take her, not even ask. She knew because she felt the same.

They hadn't discussed anything about this, he didn't know what experience she had or rather the lack of it. Would he be able to tell? Did it matter?

He had been so focused on her that she hadn't even touched or seen his hardness except feeling it against her thigh, where it felt huge. But as his knees pushed her legs aside she felt him guide it towards her. She wanted him so badly, she felt a need for him to fill her, but part of her was scared. What if it hurt? What if it was unbearable? But she didn't dare say anything. She knew she could bear anything for him.

And then he was at her entrance, slipping in, helped by her wetness, and with a firm thrust he was inside her. She tensed and couldn't breathe for a moment, the pain was so sharp. Then it eased as he began to move in and out of her and she began to relax.

He didn't know, she thought. He didn't realise, or I think he would have taken it more slowly.

But she soon joined his rhythm, wanting him deeper and deeper inside her. Squeezing muscles she didn't even know she had to take him in further, to keep him within her. Pushing against him also pressed the front of her against him, the most sensitive spot, giving her extra stimulation.

She had closed her eyes, but she opened them to see him looking at her, his eyes reading her face. When he saw her look back at him he moved his hand to brush her hair from the side of her face, and brought his lips down on hers, pausing just for a moment.

He broke off and looked at her again.

"You are so beautiful."

She felt desired and desirable. Having him, this man so much older than her, so much more experienced, want her so badly. And yet she felt doubt. Was she doing this right? Was she satisfying him?

But he made her forget these thoughts as he pressed his body on top of her more closely, shifting up, and then continued to drive into her. It made his strokes shallower but more intense, the base of him now rubbing directly against her clitoris.

Alice cried out involuntarily, and grasped him to intensify the sensation. She felt completely in his control, in his embrace. She felt complete.

And then it overtook her. Like spasms that she couldn't resist, couldn't prevent. Rocking through her, white lightning in her body, through her stomach. The desperate, aching need for him to thrust harder, faster, take her through it. She was losing herself.

She heard him catch his breath and he strained and drove into her more powerfully, two or three times, more abruptly.

Everything was happening at the same time, he was crushing her but she didn't care, grasping her so hard it would leave marks.

Then a wetness and a solution: he was dissolved into her.

They were both hot, damp, exhausted.

He withdrew and she hated him sliding out of her. It felt like she was losing him. But his lips were on hers again, tender, gentle. He murmured something that she couldn't hear and drew her against his chest.

He fell asleep quickly, she didn't sleep for some time. But she was safe, she was held. She was drained by the day, fulfilled by him, spent. Sleep lulled over her.

At some point during the night she half awoke, or realised in her dreams that she was in love with him. And she didn't even care how he felt about her. Because right now she was with him, and it was enough.

18. The next morning

In the morning, or later in the morning since it must have been nearly dawn when they had gone to bed, Alice woke. She was still in his arms, they were lying naked together. She could hardly believe she was here after wanting him for so long.

She wasn't sure how he was going to react when he woke. Would he regret it? Had he planned this? She glanced around the room trying to spot clues about his life but there wasn't a lot to see. It was a rented flat, he would only have been here for a couple of months. Still, it was his place and he must have left some mark on it.

Alice thought she must look terrible. All crumpled from sleep and no make up and her hair messed up everywhere. She wondered if she could sneak out and try and groom herself in some way. The thought of putting on last night's clothes was not very appealing as they probably had the overdose girl's vomit on them. In fact she was sure they did.

But she was trapped in his arms and if she moved he might wake. Just for now she had her own time, her own peaceful time when only she was awake. And she loved being held by him so much.

She couldn't see his face because she was at his neck level so she wriggled upwards. The movement woke him, he opened his eyes and looked at her. She hadn't studied him quite this close up.

"Good morning." He looked amazing, even rumpled from sleep.

"Good morning," she replied, relieved that he remained holding her. He obviously wasn't repelled by her morning appearance.

His arms still around her, he looked grave. "Last night, Alice, were you… was it your first time?"

She felt herself blush. Had she been that obviously inexperienced? "Yes."

He swore. "I had no idea until it was too late to stop. I just assumed… I'm sorry."

"Don't be, I don't mind. I wanted to do it." She had wanted to do it with him more than anything, to have him for her first time. But she didn't tell him this.

"I would have taken more care, gone slower. Did I hurt you?" he asked.

"No, barely. Just for a second and then it was perfect."

"It gets better." Her heart leapt when he said this. Please, please let there be a next time. She couldn't handle it if he blew cold on her again now. "But still, I shouldn't have, I wouldn't have…" he continued.

"You wouldn't have done it if you knew I was a virgin?"

"I don't know. God knows I wanted you. But probably not, not like this."

"I loved it," she told him. I love you, she thought.

"You know I've been fighting this?" he said.

"I did guess, yes." It had been very obvious. Kissing her twice in the pavilion was hardly subtle.

He pushed hair back from her face. "You are so beautiful. But also so young. I feel like I'm taking advantage."

"You're not, so please don't feel bad. I wanted it just as much. I've wanted it for weeks."

He frowned, worried suddenly. "You know that I didn't use anything? Are you ok?"

Oh god. He meant was she on the pill, which she wasn't. Why oh why hadn't she gone with Becky to the family planning clinic to get on it just in case? She had meant to but just hadn't got around to it. "I don't know. I think so." She ran some mental calculations about when she was due. "It's probably fine. I can get the morning after pill."

"If that's what you want, I can drive you wherever you need later." He ran his hand along the contours of her body as she lay on her side, down to her hip. Then he brought it over her stomach and cupped his fingers over her breast. "Right now I want you again." She could feel just how much, he was rock hard against her thigh. "But are you too sore from last night?"

She probably was but she didn't care, she wanted him inside her again so much. And if she was going to get the morning after pill they may as well go for broke.

So she smiled and kissed him lightly on the lips and moved her hand down to hold him. He twitched when she touched him. She could feel herself growing wet just at his proximity and the way his hands made her skin shiver with delight. His fingers moved between her legs, probing firmly but gently. "Tell me if I'm hurting you."

"You're not." She gasped as he flicked a finger over just the right place.

"Just there?" He increased the pressure with his thumb, moving it in a circular motion.

"Oh god yes, but stop, I don't want to... like this."

"What do you want, Alice?"

"I want you inside me." She felt kind of brazen saying it but her desire for him simply overwhelmed everything.

He moved her onto her back and pushed her legs apart. He positioned himself at her entrance. Teasing her, he wouldn't enter her fully. "How much do you want me?"

"More than anything." Please, now.

He pushed in just a little way. She was sore but she hid it, she knew the pain would be blotted out by pleasure once he was fully inside her. "Enough?"

"No, more. All of you."

He pulled out again. He was making her beg for it.

"Please, please don't stop," she said.

He smiled and teased her for a little longer, then with a smooth hard thrust that made her catch her breath he was inside her, all the way. He lay on top of her, pressed into her as deeply as he could, and she writhed her hips around to draw him in further. She loved the weight of him, his strength. The smell of his skin.

"I won't last thirty seconds if you keep that up," he warned her.

"I don't care, I can't help it." As she writhed she could rub against him so she had pressure exactly where she wanted it. He had his hands on her breasts, his thumbs brushing over her nipples. It was as though all the most sensitive parts of her body were linked by shining electric wires, everything working together with the hugeness of him inside her, so incredibly hard and deep.

Then when he thrust into her a couple more times, hard, tightening her wires it was too much and she was pushed over the edge and lost it at the same moment he did.

148

"Jesus Christ I'm like a schoolboy around you. No control."

Alice was happy regardless. She was satisfied, utterly satiated by him.

"What I want to do is take my time and make love to you slowly, so you know what it's supposed to be like," he told her. The fact he said "making love" made her feel giddy.

"It's not supposed to be like that?"

"Not that quick, no."

"We can go again then," she said.

"I need some time to recover. And so do you. Come and shower with me."

She followed him into the bathroom where the shower cubicle quickly filled with steam and hot water. Stepping in it, with him, felt wonderful. She was enveloped in it. She kissed water off his chest and neck and he ran his hands over her body before tilting her head up to kiss him. The water ran down their faces and in their mouths. It was like drinking one another.

He was soon hard again, and when she felt it she broke off the kiss and knelt down and took him in her mouth. The water was running in rivulets over her head. She was warm and drenched.

He tasted clean, warm and wet and she swirled her tongue around him. She had done this before but never really known how she was supposed to do it. He was also far larger than she had ever experienced.

He groaned, and held her head. Said her name. She really wished he would give her some direction but she went by instinct and tried to balance being firm and gentle and take him as deep as she could. Which given his size wasn't very far.

They got into a rhythm, he was rocking into her and she was trying to match it with her hands and mouth. She had her eyes shut because the water got into them otherwise, and she found it easier to focus on him with them closed.

Then he pulled away quickly. "Let's go back to bed. I want you properly."

They fell onto the bedclothes, still dripping wet, embracing. This time he went down on her, his head between her thighs. Alice had usually found it hard to relax when her ex tried this, but having just showered she felt clean, relaxed, confident, desiring and desirable.

She lay back, loving that he wanted to do this to her.

He knew exactly what he was doing. He licked up the inside of her thighs and over her sensitive folds, sliding between them. She felt his tongue inside her and it made her squirm with delight.

Then his hands were grasping her hips, pushing her onto his face as he put his mouth over her clitoris and sucked her, running his tongue over her. He kept up a rhythm that was bringing her to the brink.

He moved one hand down and pushed a couple of fingers inside her, she was so slick and wet for him that it was easy, she no longer felt any soreness from the penetration. He curled them inside her and she shuddered and gasped.

Alice had her hands in his hair, winding her fingers through it. She loved what he was doing. But she wanted him, the fullness. She pulled him up towards her and he understood.

Wordlessly, gazing into her eyes he moved over her body and pushed into her slowly, filling her completely with his length. He could go so deep it was almost uncomfortable yet she craved it. He lay there above her, looking down at her. Neither of them spoke.

He began to move in and out of her, long, slow strokes. He bent his head down and kissed her, his lips on hers, his tongue exploring her mouth and she opened to him and reciprocated. They were joined, fully joined, united.

I will never get enough of this, Alice thought. Never.

And as he increased his pace, and thrust harder and harder bringing them both to completion again, she knew her world was changed. Everything in her future would now be seen through the lens of what she felt for him. All the things she wanted, all the things she planned.

19. Exposed

When they finally got dressed he lent her a clean shirt to wear. It was far too big for her but she rolled the sleeves up. She loved the fact that she was wearing his clothes.

She sat in his kitchen while he made them coffee and toast. "Back home we'd go out for breakfast but everywhere's closed here," he said.

Alice thought she should try and check whether Jules had got back safely. She couldn't ring Jules' house because they were supposed to be together, along with Kate. If neither of them were back when she rang it would give the game away. She would have to call Becky instead.

But that could wait a little longer. Right now she wanted to stay in the bubble of just her and Mr Walker as long as possible.

"So what happens at school next week?" she asked him. She wanted to say "what happens with us?" but it might sound presumptuous and perhaps there was no "us". Maybe he would hugely regret what had happened and distance himself again.

"We'll just have to be careful, and make sure you don't call me Stewart in front of anyone," he said.

"I can call you Stewart?" The thought hadn't actually occurred to her yet.

"You can hardly keep calling me Mr Walker after last night."

Stewart. Alice and Stewart. Did this mean he did want something more? She summoned up her courage. "Do you still want to, I mean…" She was fumbling to find the right words.

"Do I want to see you again? What do you think."

Before she could reply he came over and kissed her. "Yes, Alice, I want to see you again. As unwise and wrong as it probably is."

"It's neither. I'm an adult, I won't even be in school anymore in two more weeks," she said.

"That doesn't suddenly make you the same age as me. I doubt your parents will be thrilled."

Alice didn't want to think about her parents right now. "They'll be ok. As long as I get my results and my university place anyway." And then go travelling. But that was months away. She had three whole months before then. Three whole months of summer and seeing him, if it lasted.

He put coffee and toast in front of her. She was starving. They hadn't eaten anything since Castlemorton the previous evening, and it was now nearly lunchtime. Last night seemed ages ago. Alice wondered what had happened to the overdose girl.

"Do you think she was ok? That girl last night," she asked him.

"If she was it was thanks to you. You likely saved her life."

Alice wasn't certain this was true but she liked the fact that he thought it.

"I should really ring to find out if Jules and Kate got back ok. Can I use your phone?"

"Sure." He left the room, she guessed he was being tactful so she could speak privately to her friends if she needed.

$$* * *$$

"Oh my god Alice, I have been trying to get hold of you all day, where have you been?" Becky was frantic when Alice rang her.

"What's wrong? Is it Jules?"

"No, I can't get hold of her either. It's both of you. You were on the news last night, they had a report on Castlemorton. It was only a few seconds but it was obviously the two of you. Everyone's seen it."

Jules' parents had watched the news and phoned Alice's parents, who were already shocked having seen it themselves. They had called Becky's parents to find out where Jules and Alice were, and a total meltdown was happening.

"Was Kate on there too?"

"No, it was just the two of you," Becky said.

"So no one else? Definitely just us two? And you saw it yourself?"

"Yes, who was I supposed to see? What's going on Alice, where are you?"

Alice told her. Becky started having her own meltdown. "At his house? How did that all happen?"

"I can't explain everything now. I need to get home and face the music." And she still had to get to the family planning clinic. And figure out where Jules was. Most likely she was still enjoying herself at Castlemorton, or sobering up, and would be back by evening. Alice hoped so anyway.

She hung up and went to find Mr Walker - Stewart - she still hadn't got her head around calling him that. He was in the living room.

"Everything ok?"

"Not exactly. Jules and I were on the news last night. Not you or Kate though," she said quickly, to allay his alarm.

"Are you going to be in trouble?"

"Probably. Especially if they find out that Jules and I didn't stay together and start asking questions."

But there wasn't a lot she could do about it now.

He drove her to the clinic where she was prescribed a morning after pill and a month's supply of the actual pill. A nurse gave her a kind but stern lecture on safe sex and a brown paper bag full of free condoms.

He had waited for her in the car and was amused by these when she showed him. "Different colours and everything. But the doctor said I'd be fine once I start the pill, so if you still want to then we won't have to use them."

He laughed. "If I still want to? You think I'm going to go off the idea by next weekend?" To prove it he lent over to her, slipped his hand under her shirt - his shirt - and kissed her. "I'd take you again now except I need to get you home."

"Stewart."

"What?" he asked.

"Nothing, I was just getting used to saying it."

"That's the first time you've actually said it," he told her.

"I know. It's strange, because you've been Mr Walker all along."

"Don't remind me. Except for the next couple of weeks at school. Then I never want to hear it again."

"Or Headmaster?" she said slyly.

"Not unless you want a caning."

Alice thought she possibly wouldn't mind that from him. Maybe if they went to see Basic Instinct together he might be inspired to try out that scene. She would love him to throw her over the sofa and have his way with her.

They reached her house and he pulled up on the road. "Do you want me to come in?"

"No, it will only make it worse. I don't think they'll be too mad, it's more the embarrassment of all the neighbours seeing it on TV," she told him.

He understood. "I'd like to take you out properly but next weekend is out." Fairmount's cricket team were playing in a tournament and would be staying overnight at the host school. "Are you free the following weekend?"

"It should be fine. I've got Economics the week after, but one night will be ok. If they don't ground me for Castlemorton."

"I'll see you tomorrow at school anyway."

"In the pavilion?" she asked.

He kissed her. "I think we'd better stay away from the pavilion. At least until your exams are done."

* * *

"It's not that we mind you going out darling," her mother was saying. "But we need to know where you are and that you're safe. Richard and I were very worried, and so were Jules' parents."

Alice felt all the worse that her mother was being so understanding about this. Particularly as she had no idea what Alice had really been up to.

"I assume Jules is now home safely too? Who drove you back?"

"Just a friend." Alice deliberately avoided answering the first question. She hoped Jules was back already or that she would be soon. "But don't worry, every one was sober. We only drank a few beers. We just wanted to see what it was like over there."

"It looked absolutely dreadful judging by the television news," her mother said. "Litter everywhere and very odd looking people with long hair and nose rings, in need of a good bath."

Alice refrained from mentioning that Jules was actually dating someone like this. "It really wasn't that bad. It was quite safe."

"Were there really as many drugs over there as they said on the news?" her mother asked.

"There were some. But no one forces you to take them." It always bewildered them how concerned their parents were about drugs being at a party, as though their mere presence was harmful. It was especially absurd as Cheltenham was rife with drugs. People had been offering Alice and her friends weed and other substances since they were about thirteen, not that they had the money to buy anything at that age.

"It's all the more embarrassing because Hilary Bowes' sister lives in Castlemorton village and has had all sorts of things thrown into her garden. And part of her fence was taken away." Hilary was their next door neighbour. "Now Hilary's seen you on the news being part of it, after we were only discussing the other day how awful it all was."

"We weren't doing anything like that. We just went for a look." Alice felt bad for her mother but she didn't feel particularly beholden to Hilary or her sister.

Her mother sighed. "At least you're back safely. I do worry with you being so close to finishing your exams."

Later that evening Alice's mother was putting the boys to bed and Alice was sitting in Richard's study, playing with a paperweight. She had gone in there to fetch a book but stayed.

Jules had finally called to say she was back and to vent about the grilling she'd got from her parents, but they had managed to conceal the fact that they had travelled back separately.

"What was the festival like?" Richard asked Alice.

"Very much like it looked on the news, but it's different when you're there of course."

"Was it enjoyable?"

Only Richard would ask a question in this way, Alice thought. "Yes, it was. It felt like being part of something significant, you know? There wasn't any centre, it was all spread out, but it felt..." she struggled to find the right word.

"Communal?" Richard suggested.

"Yes. I think that's it. Like it was a new society."

Richard looked for something in his desk drawer. "Many years ago some friends and I were very much into folk music. We also held impromptu gatherings. Not on the scale of the ones this summer, perhaps, but with something of the same spirit."

He brought out a few photographs. They were rather faded but they showed various people with long hair, beards and guitars at some sort of campsite in a wood, with 1960s cars and caravans in the background.

"Which one are you?" Alice asked.

"None of me, I'm afraid, I took the photos. But I did have hair like that in case you were wondering."

Alice look at the photo again and back at Richard. She found it hard to visualise him like that. "What was it like?"

"At the time it was very wonderful. We talked about a new and free society, and had all sorts of idealistic notions. It was the era of psychedelics of course."

"Did you...?" Alice wasn't sure if she should ask.

"We all did. Some of us were scientists and we regarded it rather as an experiment. The man you see on the left there became a professor of Chemistry at Imperial College. We were interested in the work of Timothy Leary and others," he said.

Alice had never heard of Timothy Leary. She resolved to look him up. "So what happened?"

"Why did we hang up our guitars? Careers and marriage and leaving university brought us back to a more conventional life. It was a brief phase, but I'm reminded of it when I see these events happening now."

PART III

Declaration

When summer brings the lily and the rose,
She brings us fear

April, William Morris

20. In trouble

"It has been brought to my attention that Fairmount pupils have attended the illegal gathering at Castlemorton in Worcestershire over the weekend."

There was a ripple of interest when the Headmaster, Mr Francis, announced this in morning assembly.

"I would like to remind you of the conduct requirements for all pupils at this school. Involvement in illegal activities, within the school grounds or outside, is absolutely unacceptable. To defy the police and the law of this country is disgraceful behaviour and the culprits will be dealt with accordingly."

Alice cursed the television news again. Out of the thousands upon thousands of people there, why did it have to be Jules and her they filmed? She could only assume the announcement was directed at them. It gave her a sinking feeling in the pit of her stomach to think about the chastisement ahead. Surely they wouldn't be suspended or anything, so close to their final exams?

She filed out of the hall behind Jules and Becky. Mr Walker - Stewart - was still outside, talking to another member of staff. He called over to them.

"Jules, about those tickets for your father for the Worcester match…"

"What tickets?" Alice asked Jules who kicked her. "Ow. Oh." She realised he was finding an excuse to speak with them. Since girls didn't play cricket at Fairmount there was no real reason for him to have anything to speak with them about.

The other teacher drifted off and Mr Walker came over.

"I don't want you both getting into trouble. I'm happy to tell the head I drove you there."

"Jesus Christ no!" Jules said. "That would escalate it from a rap on the knuckles to a disaster. We'll be fine. They'll just drone on about how disappointed they are in us and how we've set a poor example to other pupils."

"Sounds like you've been there before."

"Once or twice. It's all bark, no real bite," Jules told him.

He looked directly at Alice and she flushed, thinking of what they had spent the last couple of days doing. Back at school he seemed more remote from her, an authority figure once again. It almost seemed like a dream that this man standing in front of her had been running his hands over her naked body just 24 hours ago.

He's mine, she thought. No one knows it but he's finally mine. For now anyway.

They were interrupted by Mrs Paddington, the senior mistress, who approached them with a grim expression. "Julia, Alice, you will both report to Mr Francis at morning break. For now I suggest you stop lingering and get to your classes immediately." She nodded at Mr Walker before leaving.

Word had got around that Jules and Alice were the two illegal ravers. It was not surprising given half the school had seen the news. To Alice's amazement it had elevated their street cred. While Maddy Pullen and a few others pretended to be disgusted, there were plenty of people who were dying to know what the festival had been like.

Jules was happy to tell a few tales. She didn't really need to exaggerate the scale of things because it had truthfully been massive. Most people wanted to know about the music and the drugs and the confrontations with police.

"They did arrest one guy that I saw. But he was off his face and sitting on the bonnet of a police car trying to sell acid," Jules told them.

Morning break came all too soon and they left the Economics classroom for the headmaster's office. Alice was glad they had been summoned together. Jules didn't seem to care what happened but Alice felt apprehensive.

"How I hate this corridor. I will be glad to finally see the back of it for ever more," Jules said. During her years at Fairmount she had been summoned there for numerous misdemeanours.

Waiting outside the door was always more of an ordeal than the actual lecture. There was something about the dim light, the dark parquet and musty wood that smelled of doom.

"There's only two weeks left," Alice said. "Really, what can they do? It seems pretty pointless even calling us out."

They had already knocked and after a minor eternity the command to enter was issued from behind the door. Both girls stood in front of Mr Francis's desk awaiting the axe to fall.

"Julia and Alice, I must say that I am bitterly disappointed in you both. With mere weeks to go before you complete your time at Fairmount, you choose to disgrace yourselves and the school on national television."

"We weren't in school uniform," Jules mumbled.

"I beg your pardon, Julia?"

"No one would have known we were from Fairmount."

"That is quite beside the point. You were seen and would have been recognised by many of the pupils here and their parents, from whom I expect to receive concerned phone calls questioning the discipline and conduct of young people at Fairmount," Mr Francis said.

He hadn't actually received any complaints yet then, Alice thought. Nor would he. People had better things to do. She couldn't imagine her own mother ringing up just because she had seen someone else's child getting up to mischief in the news. Not in a million years. Mr Francis was deluded.

They had both resolved not to apologise or admit wrongdoing because neither believed they had done anything wrong. They were eighteen, they had been to the festival on the weekend not a schooldays, they weren't identifiably from Fairmount and nothing untoward had happened. Except for Jules taking drugs and Alice spending the night with a member of staff. But Mr Francis thankfully did not know these last things. "Never apologise, never explain," Jules had said. "It's what the Queen Mother does."

Alice suspected that the Queen Mother had more accommodating manners than this but it seemed like a wise strategy for their circumstance.

"Did either of you consume illegal substances at this event?" Mr Francis asked them.

What a stupid question. "I had some beer," Alice said. "Which we are legally allowed to drink."

"And you, Julia?"

Jules had had enough. She'd had enough of prissy Mr Francis over the past five years but today was the last straw.

"Unless you plan to carry out urine tests I can't see the point of you even asking that," she said.

Mr Francis looked like he was about to explode. Alice wasn't sure whether it was from Jules' defiance or the reference to urine.

Just as he started with "How dare you..." ahead of a no doubt apocalyptic tirade, Alice interrupted him.

"As you say, Sir, it's only a couple of weeks before we finish. We won't be going to another festival between now and our final exams. We understand you're disappointed but we didn't mean to end up on TV and we can't turn back the clock so unless you plan to expel us maybe we should just focus on our revision."

Mr Francis clearly had no intention of expelling them since to do so was a major move and he didn't want the newspaper headline of "Exclusive private school pupils expelled over illegal rave drugs scandal" ending up in the Daily Mail. This was inevitable whenever anyone was ousted for something juicy. The papers always got hold of it.

"I shall be writing a letter to your respective parents." As a final threat it was sadly weak.

"They already know, they saw us on TV too," Jules said.

He was losing the battle. For the first time they had less to lose than he did.

"We'll leave this matter for now. I hope you will both reflect on how your disgraceful behaviour has affected both your own reputations and that of Fairmount."

* * *

Their reputations however were greatly improved among their classmates. "We spend five years as swots, we leave as rebels," Jules said as they walked back through the school.

This was hardly true, Alice thought, since Jules had always been known as rebellious. People wouldn't have been half so impressed by the whole Castlemorton thing if Mr Francis hadn't made such a big deal about it anyway.

"It's about time we had a little talk about your antics the other night," Jules said. They still hadn't had a chance to discuss what had happened with Alice and Mr Walker in depth. All Jules knew was that Alice had gone back with him and stayed over. "It's all happening then, at last?"

"I guess so." Alice was trying to suppress the thrill of joy and excitement that came over her whenever she thought about being with him.

"Just look at your face. You've completely lost it, haven't you? In all senses of the word," Jules said.

"Maybe."

"Stop being so reticent and spill. Not every gory detail but at least an overview."

Alice did her best.

"So you're actually an item then?" Jules asked. "Alice and Stewart?"

Alice's heart sang a little at hearing their names paired. "Yes. But obviously not openly at least until school's over."

"I can't believe you ended up at the family planning clinic. I mean you're the one doing Biology, you're supposed to know about human reproduction," Jules said.

"We got carried away."

"So I gathered. At least he's good in bed."

He was more than good in bed. Even though Alice hadn't got anything to judge him by, she was certain of this.

* * *

It was even more thrilling seeing him occasionally around school. Although he seemed to be around less, perhaps deliberately keeping a lower profile, when they did cross paths he would catch her eye. They were conspirators, a secret team.

On one incredibly risky occasion when he was directly behind her in the crush of people entering the assembly hall, he fondled her from behind without anyone seeing, his hand cupping her rear.

It was only brief and Alice knew he was there but it still made her start. The thought of what he was doing without anyone else knowing, and how shocked they would be if they did know, was a huge turn on. She didn't even dare smile at him in case she gave herself away.

She sat through assembly that morning unable to concentrate on anything Mr Francis was saying. All she could think of was his presence several rows behind her, hoping that he wanted her right at that moment just as much as she wanted him.

For her part Alice didn't dare go near the pavilion or anywhere she considered to be Mr Walker's territory. As much as she was tempted she owed him at least that consideration. There was no point deliberately playing with fire. Things were risky enough already.

But it was such a rush, knowing she was seeing this man and how illicit it was. A man that so many other girls had a crush on. Sometimes she felt she wanted to shout it out.

Another time she was outside the examination hall with a group of people, waiting to go into Chemistry. He passed by and stopped to wish a couple of his First Eleven cricket players good luck. He smiled directly at her before he left and she knew his thoughts were with her.

"I'll miss seeing him about the place. First decent looking member of staff they ever get and it's only the boys who have him," one girl commented.

Alice was glad that neither Jules or Becky were there because they wouldn't have been able to resist nudging her or making some innuendo.

Maddy Pullen, jealous of the attention that Alice and Jules were getting over Castlemorton, had tried to start a rumour that Alice was dating a tramp. No one believed it but Alice let it roll. Anything that concealed the truth was a good thing.

As it was the rumour backfired, partly because Alice's, Jules' and Becky's social stars had risen that term.

"You're just bitter because you got dumped," someone told Maddy. A boy Maddy had been seeing had recently ditched her for a girl at another school, seen as evidence that Maddy's own star was waning.

It had instead got around that Alice was seeing Mike Jackson's older brother, gossip that Alice suspected Jules had nudged as much for her own purposes as Alice's. This was considered even more impressive than Castlemorton as Mike's brother had become something of a legend around the school that term. Joe was constantly getting mentioned in the local paper as "former Cheltenham boy tipped for England selection" and Fairmount was basking in his reflected glory.

"It's really unfair on Mike," Jules had said. "He should be getting the attention as captain of Fairmount's best First Eleven in decades. Instead everyone's going on about his brother."

In actual fact Joe had called Alice again. She had managed to turn him down as kindly as possible by saying that she was too busy with exams and travel plans. Not being after anything serious anyway he had taken it on the chin, but said he'd still catch up with them all for a drink next time he was in town.

Alice suspected he'd be one of those guys who would always take a chance whether a girl was available or not. He obviously liked her, but she was probably one of a string of girls he flirted with.

She just hoped the rumours didn't reach Stewart Walker's ears. She knew he wouldn't believe them if they did, but she still thought he might feel bad. Someone had made a joke about him dating Miss Symons, obviously absurd as Miss Symons reportedly cohabited with another female teacher, but it still stung Alice. She was looking forward to the day when they could just be together without all the subterfuge.

21. Date night

Finally it was the night of their first official date. Mr Walker, or Stewart as he would be for that evening at least, was picking Alice up at seven. She found she was incredibly nervous. Suddenly it all seemed official and she was worried she wouldn't know what to say to him.

She had managed to give her parents the impression that Jules was picking her up, without expressly stating it, and waited outside for him. He arrived exactly on time once again and got out to open the door for her.

Alice appreciated the courtesy but was anxious that her parents or a neighbour might see them so slipped into the seat as quickly as she could.

"How was your week?" he asked her.

"Good, now Biology and Chemistry are over."

He drove them into the town to a restaurant that was stylish without being the kind of stiff and formal place that her parents' friends went to. It was relatively new and she hadn't been there before.

As they walked from the car he had his hand against her back. "Not quite as accommodating as your other dress, but you look beautiful," he told her.

"It got kind of ripped," she said.

"I'm sorry." He hadn't wanted to remind her of her ordeal at the party.

"So you liked it then?" She hadn't been sure that he'd even noticed it. He had been pretty much the only guy there who hadn't tried groping her back at some point during the evening.

"You could say that." He cast her a glance and she saw the glint of desire in his eyes. "Your tennis gear wasn't bad either."

Alice went scarlet. "Oh god, you did see. I wasn't really thinking." She didn't want him to think she had been hanging off the tree on purpose to flash her underwear.

"It gave me plenty to think about."

They were given a prime table by the window which surprised Alice until she realised, after looking around, that they actually did look glamorous together. He was wearing a jacket perfectly tailored to his flawless physique and the dress she had chosen, while less suggestive than her backless one, was still both sexy and stylish. Most other diners were less fashionable or more casual.

While they were waiting for their orders to arrive, she asked him when he had finally decided he wanted to see her. "I thought at the party you were really angry with me."

"When I saw that idiot with his hands all over you I was so furious I wanted to knock his block off," he told her. "That's when I knew. It felt like he was mauling my girl."

"You did knock him out though, didn't you?"

"Not that piece of scum. I mean the Worcester idiot, hanging off you all the time."

He meant Joe. So he had been really bothered by it. She felt both a little bit guilty and a little bit glad. "I tried to tell you there was nothing going on," she said.

"From his side there was plenty going on."

"But I wasn't interested in him. I wanted to be with you," Alice told him.

"Yes and I'm sorry for being such a blockhead," he said. "Those guys, they're all your age. I felt like the old guy at the party."

"You're hardly that."

"I am older than you, Alice, significantly older. We can't just dismiss it."

"Well it doesn't matter for now, does it? It didn't seem to make a difference to you the other night."

They looked at one another and she knew he was remembering what had happened, just as she was. She also wanted a repeat performance tonight. Right now, in fact, but they had to get through the meal first.

But it was still too early to go home once the meal was finished. Going for a drink was risky due to the amount of Fairmount pupils whom they might bump into. Eventually he suggested the cinema which inevitably led to them seeing Basic Instinct, as nothing else worth seeing was on.

"You don't mind having seen it already?" he asked.

"No, it's the kind of film you want to watch twice, to see the clues you missed the first time round," she said.

It was even better the second time even though Alice knew who the killer was. She was slightly embarrassed watching some of the sex scenes with him next to her, not knowing what he might think of them. Or of her, for watching them twice. Maybe it would be more ladylike - more feminine - to be shocked at them like Becky was.

Outside the cinema he put his arm around her as they walked back to his car. She was blissfully happy.

"Not a bad sort, Sharon Stone," he said.

Alice had been picking up on how both he and Chris tended to understate things. It must be an Australian thing. If something was "average" they really meant it was absolutely terrible. To describe someone as "not bad" meant they were amazing.

"She is very beautiful," Alice agreed. "What about the other actress?"

"Not my type. I prefer blondes," he said, ruffling her own blonde hair. "Though she wasn't bad in that one scene."

They both knew the scene he was referring to.

"Yes that was pretty hot," Alice said. She looked him directly in the eye as she said this. Take the hint, she thought. She'd been fantasising about it for long enough.

"So you liked that did you?"

Alice felt her stomach flip with anticipation. He understood. After all, he had been pretty rough with her in the pavilion that first time and she had still responded to him. He couldn't have forgotten that.

The car was parked by a wall and before he unlocked it he turned to her and pushed her up against the brickwork. He kissed her, hard, pinning her against it. She felt the stone, cold and hard, behind her back. She could feel how hard he was through his jeans.

"You're coming back to my place," he told her.

They hadn't actually discussed whether she was staying over with him or not, but she wasn't about to refuse. They both wanted one thing right now.

He drove as swiftly as he could safely get them back to his place. Neither of them spoke on the journey back. Alice was nervous but couldn't wait to get there. After all, she had wanted this. Now she would find out if it lived up to the idea of it.

He led her upstairs and closed the door behind them. Immediately taking her in his arms he kissed her passionately for a few moments, not too roughly or enough to make her lips bleed but enough that she knew the strength of his desire.

His fingers grasped her zip and dragged it down roughly, letting her dress slither to the floor. Unfastening the clip of her bra, he let his knuckles brush against the side of her breasts. She gasped as he ran his hands over her nipples and down to her stomach, pulling her against him. Her body tingled at the feeling of his hands, warm and firm.

Then wordlessly he turned her round and bent her over the edge of the sofa, pushing down over it, just as in the film. His fingers trailed the lace edge of her underwear, then he hooked them inside and ripped them away. Her last defence was gone. She was at his mercy. Alice barely noticed the discomfort of the position as she was so turned on. She was almost embarrassed by how wet she could feel herself getting.

She straightened slightly on instinct to reduce her exposure. But he pushed her back down and gripped her hips, angling them so he had access to her. Her stomach was pressed against the hard padding of the fabric; with his superior strength and weight he was fully in control.

Then he thrust into her in one long, hard, unyielding movement.

She was ready for him but it still hurt, it was so fast and deep. She gasped but he didn't relent.

It felt like he was filling her, stretching her with every stroke. He was hitting the end of her inside which was a bit uncomfortable and she tried arching her back to reduce the depth. But he pressed back down on her, getting the angle he wanted, making it as deep and forceful as possible. She could hear his breathing, ragged, above her.

She liked it but she knew that it was about his need, his desire for her. She was bent to his will. That made her want it too, that he could want her so much. It turned her on in a strange way that she could be needed by him with this intensity: he had to have release and it had to be with her, like this, no refusal and no escape.

He reached round and slid one hand between the side of the sofa and her front. His fingers found her clitoris and pressed against it. Each time he drove into her it rubbed her against him even though he was pushing her so tightly from behind that he could barely move his hand.

This was enough to turn any discomfort she had felt into sheer pleasure. Suddenly she wanted him as deep as possible, even deeper. Hotter. Harder.

She was grinding back against him, meeting his thrusts. Her legs felt weak and she wasn't sure she could even have stood if he wasn't pinning her up with each movement.

They were both glistening and wet with sweat, out of breath.

He said her name and swore under his breath as he came, managing to bring her over with him at the same time. He was pumping into her and she cried out as the shockwaves went through her body. His orgasm seemed to last for ages. He was still thrusting after hers faded down to a heavy warmth that flushed all through her body. She felt absolutely filled and replete.

He collapsed onto the sofa, exhausted, pulling her over the side and onto him.

For a while he was unable to speak.

Eventually he asked her, "so you liked that?"

"Yes." She now felt shy. "Did you?"

"Christ Alice, what do you reckon?" He was still out of breath. "I don't think there's many blokes who would pass up the chance to throw a girl like you over and have their way."

She was partly flattered that he found her so hot but at the same time anxious that she was just a girl. As though there were any number that he would want to do this with. A thought of his ex-wife came into her mind. She'd been given the impression by Chris that she was some kind of model. How could she, just a schoolgirl, match up?

He sensed her mood change. "You ok?"

"Fine, just..." she struggled to find the right word that wouldn't reveal her insecurities. "Overwhelmed."

"You're not the only one." He stroked her face. "You'll stay with me tonight?"

That he had to ask her, that she saw tenderness in his eyes and even doubt of her own intentions, made everything all right again. It was her he wanted. At least she hoped it was.

"Yes, if you want me to."

"Want you to? I'd have you here every night if I could."

Now she felt ecstatic and went to kiss him. They made out for a while, still hot and sticky from one another and soon he was getting strongly aroused again.

This time he sat her on top of him, facing him, so she was in the position of most control. This way she could choose the pace and the depth, tease him. Which she did mercilessly. Drawing off him and resisting when he tried to plunge inside her again. Writhing her hips around.

She could push her hands in his hair, kiss his face, his neck, his chest. She loved the smell and the feel and the taste of him. She loved him.

22. In the dark

He made her a coffee and they showered together and then lay in his bed, awake. Alice was in his arms and it felt like the best place in the world. She was drowned in his warmth, his clean skin, the fresh trace of shower gel, his own male scent mingling with it.

"One week to go then?" he said.

For a moment she panicked, thinking he meant with them. Then she realised he meant school. "Yes, it's weird."

"No more detentions."

She thought of the pavilion. "We should christen the pavilion right after my final exam." Her last Economics exam was on Thursday. Less than a week from now.

He laughed. "I could still get fired. But what the hell."

"Will we still have to be discreet then? Even after I'm finished with school?"

"So long as you don't drop by to watch the cricket in your tennis skirt again, we'll be good."

Alice imagined meeting him after he'd finished coaching and blatantly going off with him in front of everyone, finally beyond reach of school rules. Imagining the look on Mr Francis's face was a very pleasant fantasy.

"I've been in more trouble this term than in the past five years," she said.

"You normally behave?"

"We normally don't get caught."

"Your dad wasn't too angry with you about the festival?" he asked.

Alice remembered Richard's surprising revelation. "No. Actually he's my stepfather, but he's great. My dad died before I was born," she explained. "Richard - my stepdad - ended up showing me some old photos of when he was a hippy. You wouldn't believe it to look at him, he's so straight and old fashioned."

"And your mum?"

Visions of an outraged Hilary Bowes floated into Alice's mind. "She was mainly worried that I was ok. And what the neighbours would think. They're pretty cool though, both of them."

"It must be hard though, not knowing your father," he said.

"Not really. It's like I don't know what I've missed. Sometimes I feel more sad for him than me. I know that probably doesn't make sense, but it was always just Mum and me. I can't imagine it any other way." She twisted round so she was looking at him. "But what about you? I don't know anything about you."

"What do you want to know?"

What she wanted to know was about his ex-wife and how it had happened and whether he still harboured any feelings for her. But she wasn't ready to ask that yet. She hoped he would tell her anyway. "How long have you known Chris?" she asked.

"Since primary school. We grew up together, played cricket together. Always had one another's backs. He was my best man."

The mention of "best man" gave Alice a horrible feeling. But it also presented the opportunity to ask him about his marriage.

"So what happened? Your divorce I mean. If you don't mind me asking," she said quickly.

"I don't mind at all. I was an idiot ever getting hitched, far too young. Chris even tried to talk me out of it on my buck's night. She wasn't the worst woman in the world or anything but it was all wrong. She wanted glamour, a different kind of life."

Alice wanted to know if he'd ever really loved her - Bree - but she obviously couldn't ask this. "How old were you?"

"Twenty-two. Just been capped, that probably had a lot to do with it. Went to my head. She made a beeline. The marriage was over for years before we finally signed the divorce papers."

All this made Alice feel a lot better. Her fears that he was pining for some beautiful Australian model who had dumped him and broken his heart could abate.

She liked lying there with him in the dark. It was still with no noises of people anywhere, just the occasional sound of a car on the street outside and the light from its headlights briefly illuminating the far wall. It was strangely powerful, the intimacy created by two people. The two of them against the rest of the world building something that was uniquely theirs.

"What about your family?" she asked.

"My father's an engineer. My mother's a legal secretary, part-time now. I've got one younger sister who's a lawyer. You?"

She considered her family. They were on a similar level to his, she thought.

"My mother doesn't work any more. She did do various things, but since having my younger brothers she hasn't. Richard does something scientific I think but I'm not sure exactly what." She explained that Richard worked at GCHQ, a government intelligence agency. "So it's all classified and no one's really supposed to know what anyone does there. I expect my mother knows though."

"And no divorces for you then?" He was joking.

"Not yet."

"I hope there won't be any for you. Divorces that is, not marriage."

Alice suddenly wondered what it would be like to be married to him. It was a strange, exciting and suffocating feeling imagining a day far in the future when he might want that. To own her and make her his, have her lie with every night, be with her always.

She didn't want to get married for years and years. But right now she also wanted to be with him for years and years. She couldn't imagine being this happy with anyone else.

She gave herself a mental kick for letting her thoughts wander in such a foolish way. After all she had only known him barely a month or so. It was amazing how much had happened in the past few weeks though. It felt like more change than she had ever known.

* * *

He woke her the next morning by kissing her. "How long have you been awake?" she asked. "What time is it?"

"Still early. But having you next to me is too distracting to go to sleep again." He ran his fingers over her body, tracing its contours. She guessed he was already hard.

"Are you going to wake me up properly then?"

Without needing further encouragement he moved over her and was soon inside her again. She adored everything he did to her and loved how much he wanted her, all the time. It was like a new power. It was the fact that despite all his reservations and all his attempts to turn her down, she had still won him over.

Against his better judgement he still couldn't resist her. And it was only getting better the more time they spent together.

Really when she thought about it she had barely known him at the start, when it was just sheer sexual attraction. But the way the other guys respected him, including Chris, people's good opinion of him, his obvious concern for her on several occasions, all this had made it so much more. Even if she didn't know everything about him yet. What his favourite book was, what music he liked, what other things he was into. But these were minor details compared his intelligence, his humour and his charisma.

And of course his incredible looks and body which happily she now had unrestricted access to.

What did he see in her though? She had never thought of herself as the kind of girl that guys went for. Becky and Jules were always encouraging her and even her mother said she had blossomed but Alice still felt quite ordinary within herself.

Her lack of experience also worried her. From his responses she figured she was doing some of the right things in bed but she didn't actually know. She was too embarrassed to ask him directly. Then there was her lack of life experience, her lack of knowledge about the world compared to his. He had lived, worked, travelled. He was educated. He knew things. She feared she must seem insubstantial to him.

"Where can we get breakfast out?" he asked her.

"We never go out for breakfast so I don't honestly know. There's a greasy spoon café in the high street that's open early in the mornings but it's pretty downmarket."

"We'll find somewhere. The weather's too good to stay indoors."

It was a beautiful morning. She was glad that he wanted to spend it with her and not send her straight home.

Then as she was in the shower she remembered her lack of clothes. Wearing her dress at this time of day would be so obviously night-before. It would be like doing the walk of shame.

His shirts were so big on her they wouldn't be much improvement, it would be clear that she was wearing his clothes. But it was better than nothing.

"Can I borrow a shirt again?" she asked him as she went into the kitchen.

"Sure. It's warm outside though."

"It's not that, it's just this dress…" she tailed off not really knowing how to describe the dilemma.

He understood. He found her another clean shirt and she put it on over her dress.

They ended up finding a café that was open along the promenade. Cheltenham was still a bit of a ghost town at this time of morning: the shops didn't open for another hour or so. Alice was never usually up this early on a weekend. It wasn't even eight o'clock yet.

A waitress brought them coffee and two breakfasts. Alice found herself surprisingly hungry given she rarely ate a lot for breakfast. There was never much time in the mornings.

She liked seeing other people walk past starting the business of their own day. There were shop workers arriving, people going for early morning dog walks, a few businesspeople who worked Saturdays. She even saw a couple of girls using a nearby telephone box who had clearly been out all night as well which made her feel better about her own situation.

She looked at him. She would start thinking of him fully as Stewart soon but it was still awkward with school. Right now he was half Stewart, half Mr Walker.

"Are you glad?" she asked him.

"Glad?"

"That you overcame your better judgement. About me I mean."

"My better judgement?" He laughed. "What a way to phrase it. But yes I am glad. Very glad."

He met her eyes directly when he said it. She was more than relieved.

"But what about you?" he asked. "Are you having regrets?"

Not in a million years. "None at all. I just sometimes feel… guilty that I made you overcome your resolve."

"I'm not some kind of monk, Alice. I wasn't breaking some sacred vow of celibacy. I just didn't want to get either of us into trouble, and you are younger than me. A lot younger than me," he emphasised.

"Would you be happier if I was thirty and divorced?" she asked.

"Probably. It would make things easier." He smiled but she could see that he was only partly joking.

As they finished breakfast he asked her about her plans for the day. "I'd like to spend the day with you but I imagine you have revision to do?"

Frustratingly, since she wanted to spend the day with him more than anything, she knew she needed to get back to her books. She was supposed to be studying with Jules some time that day. The one thing she couldn't do was let Jules or her parents down by flunking Economics at the last minute. Or herself, for that matter.

"Yes, unfortunately."

"Next weekend then. When it's all over we'll do something to celebrate."

23. Last studying

Jules seemed unhappy when Alice met her later that day to study. At first she thought it was the stress of the final exams but this would be unlike Jules since she normally breezed through Economics.

But Jules was agitated, her mind wandering. Alice had feared that she would be the one to keep getting lost in thoughts of Stewart Walker but it was Jules who was away in the clouds.

"Something's wrong isn't it? Is it Leafy?"

"No, it's all fine," Jules tried to put on a brave front but then admitted, "Actually no, it's not. He blew me off last night and I don't know why. We were supposed to go to some pub in Winchcombe but he cancelled. He didn't really give a reason or apologise."

Like the Queen Mother, Alice thought. "I'm sure it's nothing. Maybe he was tired or hungover. Or he couldn't get there. Was he with the others? Where have they gone since Castlemorton?"

It had taken the police a week to finally break up the Castlemorton festival, make arrests and move everyone on.

"They're just roaming around somewhere, I don't know," Jules said.

"What about Kate, does she know anything?"

"She's useless too. She hooked up with some guy from Bristol at Castlemorton and has been hanging out with him ever since."

Ever since was less than a week. Alice wondered how Kate's own A-levels were going.

"Was she actually seeing that guy Mush?"

"God no, he was just a friend of a friend. But what about you, what's happening with your cricket coach?"

Alice had wanted to discuss it in fine detail with Jules but now found herself oddly reticent. Partly because she didn't want to rub her joy in Jules' face if Jules was feeling miserable.

"It's ok. We went out last night and I stayed over."

This brief statement was enough to trigger huge interest in Jules.

"Again? He's really serious about you isn't he?" she said.

"I hardly think so. It's only been two weekends."

Jules was grinning now. "After the way he blew hot and cold and kept resisting you, I'd say he's fallen for you hook, line and sinker. But how do you feel?"

"I really like him of course, but it's very early." Alice could feel her face giving things away despite herself.

"Oh my god. You're in love with him, aren't you?" Jules said. "Does he feel the same?"

Alice couldn't see how he could do, given the shortness of time and the way he was still so hung up on the age gap. "I doubt it."

Jules was serious for a moment. "You know Alice to do what he's done, which is take a pretty big risk personally and professionally, I don't think he'd do that if you were just a casual shag. He obviously likes you a lot. You should think about that."

They got stuck into the macro economy and government intervention which was all absorbing for a while. Economics didn't relate much to what Alice planned to do career wise but she found it gave her a better perspective on the world. News reports made more sense than they used to.

For Jules, hoping to do commercial law, it was more relevant. Particularly the stuff on companies which Alice found least interesting. If Jules was still planning on commercial law and not planning on dropping out to travel with Leafy for the indefinite future, of course. She was so bright, it would be such a waste if she did.

Alice had once asked Jules why she wanted to do commercial law rather than criminal, which seemed more interesting to her. "Money," Jules had said. She wanted a career that was intellectually stimulating and well remunerated. Alice had envied her vision and determination.

"Does Leafy actually work?" she asked Jules. "I know he's a tree surgeon, but is he based somewhere?"

"It's more contract work. It's on and off," Jules said. Alice suspected it was far more off than on, and by Leafy's own choice.

"I wonder what will happen with Becky and Brett after the summer," she said.

"You know she's thinking of moving over there with him when he goes back to Australia?"

Alice was shocked. Becky was such a homebody and she had only known Brett for a month or so. "No way! What about university?"

"She's thinking of transferring there. The course is pretty much the same, it just costs more as a foreign student but her dad can probably afford it. They've already talked about it apparently."

Alice needed some time to process this. She had always felt sad that Becky didn't want to come backpacking with them, being less adventurous. But this was something else. Just weeks after meeting a guy she was planning to move continents?

"It's such a massive thing to do. And Becky of all people."

"I know, little old Becky. I thought she'd live within five miles of her parents' house for the rest of her life," Jules said.

"Do you think it's all a bit rushed? Is she really certain?" Alice asked.

"They're being quite sensible about it. They've got the whole summer and Australian universities start in January. So she can always defer her place here and stay with him for a few months and see how it goes over there."

It was still staggering. "She never said anything to me."

"Nor me either. I only got it out of her the other day because she was asking about how easy it would be to defer. I even thought of talking her out of it but there's something about Becky, when she's got an idea about something she's more stubborn than any of us," Jules said.

This was true. Alice sometimes envied Becky her single-mindedness even though when it was frustrating if they wanted to change her mind but couldn't. But the thought of her friend moving to Australia to live gave her a pang. It was a reminder that these days were ending, of seeing one another daily. She had taken it all for granted but of course it couldn't last forever. The three of them would be split up across the country in different universities next year either way.

"I guess we can visit her over there," Alice said.

"You'll be busy visiting someone else, won't you?"

Alice hoped so. "We haven't really discussed it. He said something once about how I should visit Sydney, but it was before all this happened."

"If you're still seeing him at the end of the summer, it's a given. I just hope you don't decide to cut Asia short and go straight to Australia," Jules said.

"Of course not! I was more worried about you ditching the trip to go travelling with Leafy."

"As if I would do that! We've been planning it for years, as if I'd let you down."

Alice was hugely relieved. "Everything just seems to be changing this term. It's not how I thought it would be."

Jules understood. "It's like it's already over, isn't it? I thought it would be a normal term, with exams, but it feels like playacting. Like they're making us do all the usual things just for the sake of it, but they've already checked out on us."

This was just how Alice felt. She supposed it made sense because there was little that their teachers could do now A-levels had arrived. They were on their own. And once they were done it was over. Biology and Chemistry were already over, no more classes, no more homework, no more revision, ever.

She said this to Jules who laughed. "If you think school was a lot of work wait until you start vet science. It'll be like A-levels but worse, every year."

At least they had a whole year off. Or a year off and three months if you counted the holidays. The thought of all that freedom was exhilarating though they'd obviously have to do some work to support themselves.

* * *

Back home Alice lay on her bed, having a rest before supper. Getting up at six o'clock or whatever it had been wasn't her usual routine. And revising was strangely tiring. She was fairly happy with how Biology and Chemistry had gone so wasn't too worried about having to get an A in Economics. Though it would still be nice to do well.

But the Becky thing - that was something to absorb. Alice looked at the photos of the three of them on her noticeboard. Were Becky's walls now covered with pictures of her and Brett?

It really was going to be the end of an era. She hoped they would all stay friends for life, but it would never be the same once school finished. Their lives were simply going to be too different.

Jules was most likely going to end up in London. Alice wasn't sure where she would be herself, it would depend on what veterinary jobs were available when she graduated, but she doubted it would be in a big city. She had also thought of working overseas. And now Becky, whom she had always imagined working in Cheltenham or at least nearby, was moving to Australia.

"Just a week to go," she said aloud.

There was no one to hear her except Ted, the large stuffed bear that had been her childhood toy and still sat on a chair in the corner of her room. He was destined to be given to her brothers when she left to go travelling.

"Did you say something, Alice?" Her mother was passing by on the landing and stopped in the doorway.

"Nothing. I was just thinking aloud, about school being nearly over," Alice said.

"Yes, it will be a big change for you all. A very exciting time though."

"Becky's thinking of studying overseas," Alice told her mother. "In Australia. She's met this guy and they're already quite serious."

Alice's mother expressed her surprise. "I wonder what her parents think?"

"I'm not sure, but from what Jules said they didn't freak out too much," Alice said.

"I suppose young people do go overseas. Hilary's nephew went to an Canadian university. His mother's originally from Canada of course." Alice's mother turned to go back downstairs. "Becky can always come home if it doesn't work out. It might be good for her to experience other cultures."

Alice wasn't sure if Australia counted as another culture. Not like China or Africa or Vietnam did. She didn't really notice many cultural differences between them and the Australian cricketers, it was more like the kind of differences you got when someone came from another county, or Scotland or something.

She looked again at her photos. What if she were to put one of her and Stewart up there? Not that she had one. Would her parents notice? Would they freak out?

If she saw him for the next couple of months they were going to have to find out at some point. Possibly even meet him. It was not a very comfortable thought.

24. Revealed

Mrs Paddington cornered Alice at the end of morning break on Monday, when she and Jules were heading to their Economics revision class.

"Alice, I'd like you to come to my office immediately."

Jules raised her eyebrows in question but Alice had no idea what was going on. Yet in her stomach she felt a kind of sinking dread.

She followed the Senior Mistress to her office which was only marginally less stark than the Headmaster's.

"Sit down please." At least the Padlock let them sit, Mr Francis always made them stand.

Not having any idea what was going on, Alice knew that she was in trouble. If something awful had happened, such as her parents being in an accident, Mrs Paddington's attitude would have been quite different.

The Senior Mistress got straight to the point.

"I have received a report that you are involved in an inappropriate relationship with a member of staff. I would like to know your response to this."

Alice was reeling. How on earth could she know? And what could she know? Her thoughts went back to Castlemorton and the news report. But he hadn't been on it, had he? Had there been another report? Had someone seen them there.

"I'm not entirely sure how to respond to that," she said. She tried to keep her voice calm but her heart was thumping and her stomach was boiling over with nerves.

"You were seen having dinner in town on Friday night with a male member of staff," Mrs Paddington said. "I require an explanation as to the nature of your relationship with him."

Had they already spoken to him? What had he said, or what would he say? Could she bluff this out?

Then suddenly Alice felt irritated. She was of legal age. Stewart Walker had never taught her. She finished school in less than four days. There was no point lying, if she had been seen she had been seen. She cursed the fact that they'd been seated in the window. It was an obvious risk - a busy street in the centre of town - anyone could have walked past.

She wondered who had sneaked. Most likely it was another member of staff as if a classmate had seen her it would have been gossip and rumours first and reached her own ears. Even someone who had it in for her like Maddy Pullen wouldn't have been able to resist digs and jibes before taking her information to a higher authority.

"I'm not sure why having with dinner with someone would be considered a matter of concern," she said to the Senior Mistress.

"You must know that it is completely unacceptable for pupils and teachers to fraternise in such a way."

Alice wanted to laugh. She thought of what they had done in his flat together being described as "fraternising". Surely that was what one did with the enemy? But she kept her face straight. Never apologise, never explain. Jules' advice would stand her in good stead here.

"I should tell you that I have telephoned your parents and requested a meeting with them. Really, Alice, your behaviour this term has been quite shocking. Just weeks away from leaving Fairmount altogether and you choose to comport yourself in this disgraceful and unacceptable way. It cannot be tolerated."

"Days," Alice said.

"I beg your pardon?"

"It's days. I finish in four days. Do you really think this is necessary?" Alice asked. She was both frightened and furious that they'd bothered her parents over this.

Mrs Paddington chose not to reply to this. "You will go and work quietly in the reading room." The reading room was a currently unassigned classroom used for a range of purposes.

"I can't go back to class?"

"Under the circumstances I don't think it is appropriate that you come into contact with other pupils."

So she was some kind of leper. Probably about to be expelled. She followed Mrs Paddington to the reading room and sat down at a desk. She wasn't at all sure how she could concentrate on any work now but there was little else to be done.

* * *

Sitting by herself in the reading room Alice felt strangely calm. It had had to come out sometime. At least she knew where she stood with Stewart now, that he liked her and wanted to continue seeing her. She didn't think that exposure this late in the day would make him change his mind. After all what was the point of ending it now? The worst had happened.

She desperately wanted to see him and find out what was happening with him. Would they sack him? She rather thought they wouldn't because the scandal would be too great. After all it was just a few days and then it didn't matter any more. Surely they couldn't be that set on a point of principle?

Alice thought of the boy who had been expelled for drugs not long before his A-levels. Maybe she'd have to sit her own exams in jeans. There were only two papers left, tomorrow's exam and then the final one on Thursday, so it wasn't too horrendous a prospect.

There was a knock at the door and it opened. She was startled to see Richard there. He didn't look furious or disgusted, so that was something.

"I asked to see you before I spoke to your Headmaster," he said. "Are you alright?"

"I'm fine. Did they tell you what it was about?"

"Rather briefly and with odd phrasing over the telephone. I thought I would like to hear your side first," he said.

Somehow Richard made it easy for her to tell him. He was such a factual person. She explained about the dinner. "He's not actually my teacher, he's coaching cricket and he only joined this term. He's a friend of Becky's boyfriend." This was true but also a much more palatable way to put it, Alice thought.

"Is he rather older than you?"

Alice met his eyes directly. She didn't want to lie to him. "Yes, he is," she admitted. "And he was very reluctant at first because of that. In fact he kept his distance as much as possible and it was me who kept trying to persuade him."

"I see. Is he the sort of man that your mother would find acceptable?"

This question threw Alice somewhat because she had never really considered it.

"Yes I think so. Not given his age, perhaps. But if she and you were to meet him socially, I think you would both like him."

"Then that should probably be arranged. But for now we'd better go and deal with your Headmaster."

Alice marvelled at Richard's attitude. She had thought he would at least disapprove or show disappointment in her, but he seemed very neutral. Admittedly he'd never been angered with her or disciplined her as long as she could remember, though she had never really given him occasion to. The minor misdemeanours she got into around the house, such as leaving her laundry in the wrong place or staying out later than she had promised, were things her mother usually dealt with.

"You want me to come with you?" she asked.

"Yes. I don't think there's any point them seeing me separately. I have nothing to say on the subject that can't be said before your ears, and I only know as much about it as you have told me."

He meant they should put on a united front even if he didn't say it. Having dreaded her parents arriving, Alice now looked on Richard as some kind of champion.

* * *

A formal and awkward meeting was held in the Headmaster's office, with both Mrs Paddington and Mr Francis present. Alice and Richard sat opposite them, Richard having drawn out a chair for Alice with his usual courtesy. Mr Francis would have expected her to stand but he could hardly ask her to do so now. It would look absurd after Richard's gesture.

"I thought it would be useful for both Alice and I to attend this meeting and resolve this matter," Richard said. Alice had never seen Richard in a situation like this. He took a quiet command in a way that clearly disconcerted the two teachers opposite them.

"So the issue before us is that Alice was seen having dinner on Friday night with a member of your teaching staff?" Richard said.

"As you must be aware," Mr Francis said, desperate to regain ascendancy, "inappropriate relationships between pupils and teachers at Fairmount - at any school - are unacceptable."

"And it is your view that having dinner constitutes an inappropriate relationship?" Richard asked.

"Fraternising in private with a member of staff is absolutely inappropriate."

"I see. So with just four days of Alice's time at Fairmount remaining, what course of action do you propose?"

Mrs Paddington glanced at Mr Francis. Alice could tell they were both furious but also uncomfortable. This was thanks to Richard.

"In the normal course of events Alice should face immediate expulsion," Mrs Paddington said.

"Which could not of course preclude her from completing her exams, even if other arrangements were required," Richard said. Alice wasn't sure how he knew this. "How many classes do you have left, Alice?"

Having now missed the today's session she had only one class left, an Economics revision class on Wednesday morning. The more she thought about it the more absurd this whole situation was, Alice thought. Why on earth didn't they just overlook it and let it go?

"Arrangements can be made for teaching notes from that class to be sent on," Mr Francis said.

Richard frowned slightly. "Might it be reasonable to suggest that Alice's exclusion from Fairmount might distract other pupils at a time when you would doubtless prefer their full attention to be focused on their studies?" he said.

"I'm not quite sure what you mean," Mr Francis said.

"And the publicity that so often results from these situations, always a considerable disruption throughout the school and wider community," Richard continued.

He had hit their weak point. Bad publicity was the last thing they wanted.

"Alice has, as I am sure you would agree, been an exemplary pupil at Fairmount as her future career plans demonstrate. Without wishing to employ the cliché of mountain and molehill, surely the most sensible course of action, given no actual illegal act has occurred, would be to allow her to finish her exams and farewell the school in due course."

Mr Francis shifted in his chair. He really was a weaselly little man, Alice thought. Mrs Paddington's lips were set in a tight line.

"I think Mrs Paddington and I will discuss this between ourselves," he said. "If you would care to wait outside for a short while, we will inform you of our decision as quickly as possible."

Alice knew she and Richard had won. But Mr Francis wanted to present their victory as his idea and his judgement. They returned to the reading room.

"This should take all of five minutes," Richard said, looking at his watch. They sat there in companionable silence, each lost in their own thoughts.

Sure enough within ten minutes Mrs Paddington reappeared. "If you will come this way once again," she said.

Alice's hopes were realised. Mr Francis uttered a stuttering, pompous little speech about exceptional circumstances and granting Alice the special privilege of being allowed to remain at Fairmount, with the condition that she was to have no contact with the male member of staff in question within or outside school until the school term was complete. Which, Alice calculated, was in about seventy-two hours time.

25. Scandal

Alice walked with Richard back to his car. She may as well have gone home now since there was only lunch and an unsupervised revision session that afternoon. And tennis, but most people skived off now with the excuse that they were revising. The games mistress had finally given up on them.

And it was a glorious day. The kind of day for not being in school, stuck in a classroom.

"Thank you so much for everything you did," she said. "I am very sorry, I really didn't want to upset you and Mum."

Richard turned to her. "Naturally your mother is somewhat shocked and anxious, Alice. For my own part I was surprised but all things considered, I have every confidence in you. You have always been responsible and excelled throughout school, and there doesn't appear to have been any disruption to your exams."

Alice felt both uplifted and slightly ashamed by this, as she hadn't been upfront with them about a lot of things recently.

"I'd never jeopardise that."

"I am sure you wouldn't." Richard stopped to talk to Alice before he opened his car door. "It's an unusual time, the end of school. Legally you are of course all adults but remain constrained within the school environment. I've often wondered if a less structured approach would be more appropriate. Easier perhaps for both teaching staff and pupils to strike a balance between rules and freedom."

Alice agreed. "Last year wasn't so bad. But this year it seems that we do a lot of things for the sake of doing them."

"I suppose the school needs to keep some form of order and routine. Don't worry about your mother, I will assure her that everything's fine."

He drove off leaving Alice feeling rather stranded. She didn't really know what she should be doing. She didn't really want to show up half way through the Economics revision class to a load of inquisitive eyes.

She was relieved that Richard had saved the day but also strangely deflated. It was as though she had been offered a sudden glimpse of sheer freedom which was now snatched back. If they had expelled her she could have gone anywhere, done anything right now. As it was she had to go back to school and keep her head down.

Still, just a few more days and she would finally be free.

* * *

Jules and Becky cornered her at lunch, wanting to know what had happened. They were shocked when Alice told them.

"I wonder who can have seen you?" Becky asked.

"Someone prepared to sneak," Jules said. "Most likely a teacher I would think. I can't imagine anyone else reporting it except for someone like Maddy."

Alice thought the same. "I don't think it was Maddy though because she would have given me looks earlier today and she didn't. I'm sure it was a member of staff. I suppose they had to report it if they saw us."

"What's happened to him, has he been fired?" Becky asked.

Alice had been worrying about this. "I have no idea. I haven't seen him all day."

"I bet he won't be," Jules said. "After all, he's not quite a teacher, is he? And they need him for the cricket, the First Eleven are doing amazingly. It would be such a scandal if they fired him. They couldn't hush it up because parents would ask where the coach was."

It was true that Stewart Walker had transformed Fairmount's cricketing fortunes. For a school that took pride in sport this made him very valuable.

Alice considered how awful it would be for him if the cricket team found out. He'd been annoyed enough when the Gloucester team were having a go. But if the boys he actually coached knew he was seeing one of their classmates it would be far worse.

"I shouldn't worry. He's pretty tough, he'll just brush it off. Besides they wouldn't dare make remarks like Graeme and the lads do," Jules said.

"I hope so." Alice was getting a better idea of why he had held off for so long. She hadn't really considered the consequences seriously enough. Exposure for him was far worse than for her.

"I just can't believe Richard came good for you like that," Jules said. "He always seems so detached."

"He notices more than you might realise," Alice said. She had only started realising this herself recently. Richard gave the impression of being removed from mundane things but he was still very observant and aware of what was going on.

"Anyway, I'm absolutely banned from going anywhere near him - Stewart - for the next few days. So I daren't even find him to ask him if he's ok."

"If you're banned from seeing him then it's all the more likely he hasn't been sacked," Jules said.

Becky suggested that they could go and find him on Alice's behalf.

"Better not, he'll probably want to keep well away from us all for now," Jules said.

The conversation moved on to other things. There was a leaving party being held at Gas, a local nightclub, on the Friday night, not just for Fairmount but for school leavers from other schools too. Becky was keen for everyone to go as it would be the last time that many of their other school friends were all together. Jules had reluctantly agreed as Leafy apparently hadn't made any arrangements with her for that night.

Alice was torn between going and seeing Stewart.

"Do both. Go to his place afterwards," Jules suggested.

"You can't miss it," Becky said. "I know it's only Gas but everyone will be there."

They were also planning what they would do with their time after next week. Alice would be working more shifts at the veterinary surgery throughout the summer to save more for her gap year trip. Becky's father had got her a part time job in a nursing home. Jules was angling for a job in a bar but these were rare and hard to get at this time of year, since university students were returning home for the holidays and usually grabbed them all.

"So much freedom!" Jules said. "Literally no one telling me what to do any more."

"Except for your parents."

"They'll ease off assuming I get all my A-levels."

"The results don't come out until August," Becky said.

Alice wondered what the wait was going to be like. Once the euphoria of finishing the last exam and leaving school had died down, would it hang over their summer like a dark, oppressive cloud? They would have to find some way to forget about it. Focusing on a really solid Plan B might help.

But she didn't really want to do anything except veterinary science. Plan B was repeating her exams and having a second shot, though that also mean saying farewell to her travel plans. And to visiting Australia.

* * *

Back home Alice braced herself for the worst. Her mother, as she had anticipated, was more worried than angry. And more angry with him than with Alice.

"What kind of a man can he be, Alice, to go after a girl your age?"

Alice tried to explain that Stewart was the one who had held off while she had pursued him, but her mother was unconvinced.

"He still had a choice. Divorced as well. Why can't you find a nice boy your own age?"

The fact was that Alice hadn't really been looking for anyone. What with A-levels and her summer plans, it was the worst time to meet anyone, least of all seriously. She tried to explain this to her mother.

"This just happened, and I didn't know I was going to feel this way. But it doesn't change anything. I'm not about to emigrate like Becky is," Alice said.

Her mother was not convinced. "Richard thinks we should meet him and I agree. You may be eighteen and free to do what you like, but while you live here we would like to be aware of who your friends are. We'll have him over for dinner next week."

Alice really did not want this. She imagined it could only be hideously awkward but she didn't have much choice.

"I'll see if he's free."

"I just hope this hasn't affected your exams," her mother continued. "You know how important this term is. You're far too young to be dating this man, especially at a time like this."

It was no point arguing the last point. "My exams are going fine, honestly," Alice said. "We revised exactly the right material for Biology and all the questions I was hoping for came up. And Chemistry was fine too."

Her mother looked at her. Her face showed her usual love but also concern. It made Alice feel guilty as she hated worrying her mother.

"I just don't want you to be unhappy, darling. Something like this can't end well."

"Why not?" Alice asked.

But her mother wouldn't give a reason. "Let's meet him first and we'll talk about it later."

He rang her later that evening and fortunately Alice was the one who picked up the phone. It was in the hall which gave her some privacy.

"How are you? I wanted to see you earlier but I was worried it would get you into more trouble. What did the Head decide?" he asked.

She loved hearing his voice. His accent, his tone. After one of the worst days of her life she no longer felt alone. "I'm not expelled. Nearly, but Richard - my stepdad - saved the day. I'm completely forbidden from any contact with you though. At least until after Thursday."

He laughed. "I think I can possibly wait that long."

"What about you? They didn't fire you?"

"No. A rap on the knuckles, though I offered to resign."

Alice asked if Mr Francis had told him who had seen them.

"He just said 'one of the staff'."

Exactly as Alice had thought. It would have been all round school if it had been another pupil, though probably would be by Thursday anyway. These things always got out. She wasn't sure how she felt about everyone knowing, but so close to the end of term maybe it didn't really matter.

"I'm sorry I couldn't be there for you," he said.

She told him it was fine. She was just happy that he had wanted to be there though she didn't tell him. "Another thing, my parents want you to come over for dinner next week." It was a statement not an invitation as she was anxious he would refuse.

"Which day?"

Alice felt hugely relieved. She wasn't sure how she had been expecting him to respond but he sounded as though he didn't even see it as a problem. But she thought she should better warn him. "They want to check you out."

"Of course they do. I'm thankful it's dinner and not a shotgun."

Once again she was relieved and impressed by how he just took things in his stride. Nothing seemed to faze him. "So do all the other staff know?" she asked him.

"Not that I know of. I'm sure word will get around," he said.

She felt bad. "I'm sorry." After all, she got to escape in a few days. He still had to face everyone.

"It's not your fault. And in case you're worried, I don't regret a thing."

Something in his voice thrilled her but also scared her a little. It was the enormity of it all, what she had brought them both to. She wished she could be with him now so he could put his arms around her and make everything ok. She wanted to close her eyes and shut out the rest of the world. How she longed for this week to be over.

26. Dumped

The first Economics exam on Tuesday went reasonably well. So Alice was surprised when Jules wasn't in school on Wednesday. It was their last Economics revision class before the final exam so where on earth was she?

No one at school seemed to know, and as Alice was trying to keep a low profile herself she didn't like to ask any of the teachers.

So she went round to Jules' house after school to discover Jules a tear-stained lump of misery in her bedroom, with all the curtains closed.

"What's wrong? You weren't on the sick register."

"I'm not sick, I'm broken," Jules said.

It was Leafy. Unbeknownst to Jules he had also been seeing another girl and had been quite blithe about it when Jules found out. "Apparently he thought I would have known. Free love or some such bullshit like that."

Alice, who had been fearing that Jules had got pregnant or something worse, was privately slightly relieved.

"Maybe that's just what all those people do," she said.

"Her name was Petal, can you believe it? Not Petal like a nickname or something, I mean her parents actually christened her that. Petal. What a stupid name." Jules was working her way through a large box of tissues that were crumpled all over her bed.

"Is she a crusty?" Alice asked.

"No, even worse, she looks totally normal. I met her once, before I knew he was screwing her. She's all petite and perfect with glossy dark hair. She looks like that girl off The Wonder Years." Jules herself was tall and her reddish brown hair defied most styling. Alice thought she had beautiful hair, it was so thick and wavy, but Jules had always wished it was straight and sleek.

"She lives on a canal boat, for god's sake," Jules continued. "In Tewkesbury. And she has a kid."

It was unclear from her tone which of these things offended her the most.

"It's not his though? The kid?"

"God no. Not unless one of his ancestors is a Rasta or something."

At least this meant any of Jules' plans of joining the alternative community and ditching her degree were hopefully over as well.

"You could still do something environmental, you know. Maybe specialise in environmental law?" Alice said.

"Sod that. Working pro bono for a logging company is more like it."

Alice went to open the curtains. "It's a really nice afternoon. Come out for a walk."

Jules vowed she was never going out in daylight again.

"You can become a recluse after tomorrow. Just one more exam. Let's go to the garage for some chocolate and then we can go through the notes from today's class."

There was a petrol station two streets from where Jules lived. Open 24/7 it was a popular snack stop after a night out.

Reluctantly Jules dragged herself up. "I look like hell. I haven't got any make up on."

"Just wear sunglasses."

Jules obeyed which was rare for her. She truly was broken down, Alice thought.

Outside the weather was flawless. Surely this would lift Jules' spirits.

"I never asked about how you were going," Jules said. "Anything more happen regarding your lover boy?"

It had been a huge relief to Alice that even if all the staff knew none of the pupils had managed to find out. She was pretty sure she had detected certain glances and looks of disapproval from various teachers though it could have been her paranoia imagining it. But if it had got round the school she would have had grief from Maddy and other. Happily they had said nothing.

"You got very lucky then. Though I suppose it doesn't really matter now," Jules said.

"Still embarrassing with all the staff knowing, if they do. I always thought it would be cool if they found out but somehow it all makes me feel like That Girl."

"Most are probably jealous," Jules said. "He's the best looking staff member at Fairmount in years. Possibly ever. Pretty galling that he's seeing a sixth former rather than one of them."

They crossed the road to the service station. Mid-afternoon, in the early summer heat, everything seemed hazy and quiet. There weren't any cars there filling up.

"That's what I thought it would be like. But it's not, it's as though they think less of me," Alice said.

"I shouldn't worry about it. I bet most of them don't even know. Francis and the Padlock would want to keep it hush if they didn't actually expel you."

Much chocolate and revising later, Alice returned home. She was feeling fairly relaxed about the final exam tomorrow. And also excited. It was a bit like Christmas Eve: waiting for the very last day of school.

One more exam, and then... nothing. Some of the other Economics students were planning to go to a nearby restaurant with a licensed bar for lunch and start the pub crawl early. Alice had other plans.

At least Jules was in a better mood by the time Alice had left. With luck the loss of Leafy wouldn't drag down her entire summer.

Her mother was making supper when Alice entered the kitchen. "Did you find Jules?" she asked. "Was she ill?" Alice had stopped home briefly to change out of her school uniform before heading to Jules' place.

"Yes, and no. Sort of. She had a heartbreak thing going on," Alice said. "But she'll be fine for tomorrow. You know Jules." Jules was resilient.

Her mother sighed. "You girls. Why can't you all just finish your exams and leave the complications for later? You have all the time in the world."

But it just didn't work like that. Things happened when they happened. Neither Jules, Alice nor Becky would never have planned to fall headlong in love in the middle of their A-levels if they had any control over things.

Alice remembered someone once telling her that you always met someone the night before you went on holiday. Or at a leaving party. Either because it was Fate throwing a spanner in the works or because you gave off a special unavailable vibe that made you irresistible. In actual fact Alice didn't think it was either of these things. It was simply bad timing.

"It all just happened," she said. Not without a twinge of guilt since she knew she had actively pursued Stewart.

There were a lot of what ifs. What if he hadn't kissed her in the pavilion that first time, might she have given up? What if he hadn't been at the barbecue? What if he'd never come to the rave at Selsley? Actually the more she thought about it, it was as much him as it was her.

This wasn't something she planned to tell her mother though. "Is Richard back?" she asked.

"He's in his study."

Alice still felt she owed Richard hugely for his role with Mr Francis and Mrs Paddington that week. She wasn't really sure how to repay him. But that currently mattered less to her than his good opinion. It wasn't something she had thought about before but now she was worried he thought less of her.

Richard looked up from some papers as she hovered at the door. "Ready for the final day?" he asked.

She took this as an invitation to come in and sit down. "We've revised everything possible. I just have to try not to forget it overnight."

"I'm sure you'll do admirably. Your mother and I are both very proud of how well you have always done at school. Whatever your results come August, you have a bright future in front of you."

This meant a lot coming from Richard. Her mother was modest about his virtues but Alice had come to realise over the years that he was very highly respected in his field and possibly even brilliant. This was despite never knowing exactly what he did. The research he carried out in his study was for his private interest since he couldn't bring his actual work home.

She wasn't really sure what to say except to thank him.

"I always wanted a daughter," he told her. "I realise I can't take the place of your own father but I feel very blessed to have you as well as the boys."

Alice was unexpectedly moved. He had always just been Richard to her, an uncle-like figure whom she was very fond of. She had barely seen him as a stepfather let alone a father.

"I never knew my father so there isn't really a place to take," she said. "My mother and then you are all I've really known." She hoped this conveyed what she wanted it to.

He smiled, so hopefully it had.

"If you are ever in trouble I hope you will feel able to let me know. Should you run into financial difficulties on your trip, for example."

Alice could see that there was something that he didn't feel quite able to say but she guessed what it was. He didn't want her feeling that she had to rely on Stewart or anyone else, that he and her mother were still there for her.

"I will, I promise." She suddenly felt incredibly lucky. There were so many choices and options in front of her but they were good choices. She was safe.

27. Final day

"School's out!"

Jules and Alice were finally done. Becky had finished a couple of days earlier, but she was meeting them at the school gates to celebrate along with the rest of those who had just finished Economics. They were off to the nearby restaurant and happy hour lunchtime cocktails.

Alice was a few minutes late, and when she showed up she was wearing her tennis gear. "I'll join you guys in a while. I have something to do first."

"Oh god you are not doing what I think you are doing. I thought you were joking about it," Jules said.

Alice grinned. "It's the last time I'll ever be wearing this, so it may as well get a send off."

"Does he actually know what you have planned?"

"Maybe. He'll soon find out anyway."

Everyone else was so absorbed by the thrill of finally finishing school that there weren't any more questions and Alice slipped away.

As she had expected, Stewart was over by the nets preparing for the afternoon's cricket practice. His eyes widened when he saw her. "Is that what you wore to your Economics exam?"

"I thought I should say a final farewell to the pavilion," Alice said.

"Do you need some assistance with that?"

"I think so."

He went inside with her and locked the door behind him. "Christ those skirts are distractingly short," he said as he turned her to face him.

Alice felt inexplicably nervous. Even though she couldn't really be expelled now, and there was little chance of anyone trying to get in the pavilion anyway at this hour, it felt like a huge transgression of the rules.

Here they were once again, in the dark cool of the pavilion, with its musty smell of summer and sports. Her last taste of school.

He cupped his hand on her rear, his fingers reaching under the edge of the fabric. He stopped, and then moved his hand a little further. "You're not wearing anything under this?" He was shocked but desire flickered in his eyes. She felt him caress around the curve of her rear, feeling her bare skin.

"Not exactly."

"A fine sight for Mr Francis if the wind blew it up in front of him." He was clearly as amused as he was turned on by her lack of underwear. He drew his hand between her legs as he put his other on her shoulder and brought her to him.

She could never get enough of kissing him. His lips were firm and warm, he knew just the pressure to use to tease her own lips and gently bite down her neck, into the sensitive hollows above her collarbone.

She reached for his own clothes, trying to undo his fly, but he stopped her. "I won't last more than a few minutes as it is."

"You want it that badly?" she asked, delighted by his desire for her. She felt the same. The ban imposed by Mr Francis on any contact between them for the past few days had only made her obsess with longing for him.

"You walk in here like every man's fantasy, half-naked in that outfit, how long do you expect me to last?"

She laughed and then shuddered as his fingers slipped inside her, where she was already unbelievably wet for him.

"Seeing as you've made yourself so conveniently accessible..." he turned her round and pushing up her tennis skirt she felt him position himself between her legs. He was rock hard. He had her facing the wall, and she put her hands against it for balance.

He pushed into her and she caught her breath. She felt the warmth of his chest against her back, his hands slipping beneath her shirt feeling for her breasts. She loved him touching her body, how his hands felt caressing her. Strong and warm. Knowing just how much he wanted her.

She felt him inside her: the perfect fit. He felt it too. "We fit so well, you're perfect." Hearing him say this made her body ring with pleasure and increased her own desire for him.

"Do you want me as much as I want you?" he asked.

"More. Endlessly."

He laughed, out of breath. "I can't go forever, it's hard holding off at all given what you do to me."

This inspired Alice to try and make him lose control. She writhed her hips back against him, loving how the change of angle felt, trying to draw him in even more.

"You do that again and I won't last another second." His hand stroked down her stomach and his fingers slid to her most sensitive place. This made her arch involuntarily. "You're going to come with me," he told her.

His fingers kept up the pressure, firmly and relentlessly moving over her. She cried out and squirmed against him. He had complete control of her body.

Here she was, her last day of school, with the school cricket coach screwing her in the pavilion. The forbiddenness of it and the thought of what the Headmaster would do if he knew sent a momentary thrill through her.

But he wasn't just a cricket coach. He was hers. She didn't know if she could call him her boyfriend but she was with him, properly. They didn't have to hide any more.

The rhythm of his fingers and his thrusts inside her were exactly right. She needed this and she needed him. She nearly cried out how she felt - that she loved him, that she was in love with him, that she could never imagine anyone else making her feel this way - but she didn't quite dare yet.

Instead she bit her lip and tried to muffle her own sounds as he brought her over the edge and the pleasure radiated out of her from where he was touching her, inside and outside.

She heard and felt him orgasm too, triggered by her own climax. He was saying her name and gripping her against him.

Then he pulled her upright and around to face him, and his lips were on hers, passionately and tenderly. "You are the best. You're like an addiction," he told her between kisses.

She didn't know if she really was the best but she loved that he said it.

"So now the ban on contact with you is lifted, when am I seeing you next?" he asked.

She wanted him to come to the restaurant with her. But with half the First Eleven there it would likely be awkward. He would still be coaching some of them even after exams were over as there were several matches left before the official end of term.

"Tomorrow night there's the leavers' party..." She knew he couldn't come to that, but she didn't think she could wait another whole day to see him.

"Can you come round afterwards?"

"It might finish late." She looked at him expectantly, hoping the invitation would still be open.

"If I'm asleep you can wake me up." His eyes told her all she needed to know. He wanted to be with her.

She answered him with a kiss, moulding her body against his and feeling the wonderful hard planes of his chest and the muscles of his back. She could feel him start to grow hard again.

"I could make love to you all afternoon but at some point we'll have the Second Eleven banging at the door for nets practice. They might prefer a show but I'm not planning on giving them one," he said.

Alice laughed. "OK. I'll leave you be."

"And you'd better put something on under that," he said, feeling her bare flesh under her skirt again. "I want you open access to me, but not the whole world."

No one had ever expressed anything like possessiveness to her before. While Alice knew he was joking, she loved the sense of being his and his alone.

He kissed her again and she slipped back to the main school to shower and change. She no longer cared what anyone might think of her being in her tennis gear in the middle of the day. She was free and she could do what she liked.

* * *

The others were still on drinks and hadn't ordered food yet when she arrived at the restaurant. There were about twenty people there from school including Becky and Jules. It was an American diner themed outlet with a huge cocktail and beer menu.

"What took you so long?" someone asked. "Get a last minute detention?"

"Something like that." She was feeling incredibly happy.

"A detention in the pavilion," Jules said. She was already half wasted, there were huge communal jugs of Long Island Iced Tea on the tables that had no doubt contributed.

"In the pavilion?" Oh god, Maddy Pullen was there, her ears instantly pricking up.

"Yeah. Alice had a sporting engagement." Jules was grinning, she no longer cared what Maddy knew or thought. In her drunken state anything that annoyed Maddy was a score worth making.

Alice did care. She kicked Jules under the table though she doubted it would do much good.

"What do you mean?" Maddy asked. She wasn't going to let up.

"Are you taking up cricket?" a boy asked, getting the wrong end of the stick.

"No, I just had something to do. But I'm here now and ready to get some drinks in," Alice said, hoping to change the subject.

But cogs were turning in Maddy's mind. "You weren't with him, were you? Don't tell me you went and flung yourself at him. There's no way he'd be interested in you."

"You said that before," Jules reminded her. "And you were wrong then just as you are now. Because he is interested in her, and they've been together for some time."

"Jules!" Alice hadn't bargained on being exposed by Jules' drunken defence. She wished Becky would help her out but Becky seemed even less sober than Jules and was barely communicating.

Maddy didn't want to believe it. "There is no way. There is just no way," she kept saying.

"What's going on?" someone else asked.

Maddy turned to him. "Jules is trying to claim that Alice is seeing Mr Walker, but it's bullshit."

"Seriously? The coach?"

Everyone was now fixated on the conversation and Alice was blushing red.

"You're going out with Stewart Walker?" It was one of the First Eleven. There was no hope of keeping it under wraps now. Not that Alice needed to but she hadn't quite been ready for some huge announcement either.

"Not exactly." She was she supposed, but it hadn't quite been put into those terms. She caught Mike Jackson's eye and felt a twinge of guilt. He hadn't said anything but he clearly knew something about the situation, doubtless from Joe.

"He's old enough to be your dad, isn't he?"

"If Francis found out he'd go ballistic!"

Maddy was furious. "You are such a slag."

Without warning a half-full jug of cocktail was tipped over Maddy's head. "What the hell?" she said, turning round in a fury, liquid streaming from her hair and slices of fruit all over her.

It was Becky. Quiet little Becky, liberated enough by alcohol to reach the end of her tether.

"You are the slag, Maddy. You slept with that guy from Malvern High and that's why Paul Sutton dumped you," Becky.

Maddy swore at her.

But now it was Becky who wouldn't let up. "I'm so sick of you having a go at all of us all the time when you are the biggest hypocrite out there."

Someone started chanting "cat fight!" but Maddy took one look at a fairly aggressive looking Jules sitting next to Becky, and a sober but angry Alice, turned on her heels and marched off.

"Good riddance," Becky said. Alice then wanted to laugh. Anyone else would have said something far stronger.

The row and the sight of a drenched Maddy and her exit fortunately reset the mood and took the focus away from Alice's love life. Someone slammed an empty jug on the table and shouted "drinks!"

"I will kill you later," Alice said to Jules under her breath.

Jules grinned again. "No you won't. Who cares about this lot, we're free. At least that bitch finally got it. And from Becky too."

It was probably true that there wasn't really any damage left to be done. Alice's parents already knew, the Headmaster knew, what did it matter if the whole world knew? Someone would probably see them out on the town sooner rather than later anyway. After all a teacher had already spotted them the one night they had gone out together.

"I owed you one," Becky said. "You got a detention for my sake."

Alice thought back to the clean-up. "I probably owe you for that, given how it turned out."

28. Leaving party

Gas was a thick fug of sweat, cigarette smoke, beer and bodies when the three of them arrived for the leavers' party. The music pounded so loudly that conversation was nearly impossible from the moment they were through the door.

At Becky's suggestion they were all dressed up. Half the people there were in jeans and Doc Martens and half in club wear. "We might be able to queue jump if we look really glam," she said.

"I don't think the bouncers will care tonight, given it's all school leavers and ticketed," Jules pointed out.

But Becky was right. The queue stretched around the block by the time they arrived so they marched up to the door. "Priority tickets," Becky announced.

"Let's have a look," the bouncer said, but he paid more attention to Becky's skin-tight dress than the regular ticket she held out to him. He waved them through to the scowls of some gothic looking people still waiting at the front of the line.

"What has got into Becky? What a score," Jules said.

But Alice knew why Becky had changed. It was Brett. She was happy and secure and it made her more confident. Becky had also got used to being given priority entry to places when she was with him. Being county cricketers made them minor celebrities in the places they tended to frequent.

"To the bar then. We get one free drink with this ticket."

There was a real spirit of camaraderie in the club that night, both with people from school that they'd not really been friends with before, as well as with people from other schools. Old differences were forgotten. Everyone was upbeat. Everyone was celebrating. It reminded Alice of the euphoria at Castlemorton.

The rave scene had cooled sharply since the illegal festival had eventually been broken up. There had been several arrests and some people were talking about moving over to Europe, according to Kate.

Glastonbury was in a couple of weeks but many travellers were complaining that it was getting too commercial. This inclined Jules to go, since it meant Leafy wouldn't be there, but fifty quid for a ticket was a bit heavy when they were saving for their overseas trip.

"I wish you were coming backpacking with us Becky," Alice said, not for the first time.

"I almost would, I think, except for going to Australia with Brett."

"We could all meet up for Christmas. We should be in Australia by December," Jules said. "Brett can get us tickets for the Boxing Day test. My dad would never forgive me if I was in Melbourne and didn't go."

Alice thought about Stewart. Would she still be with him then? She hoped so. They might be taking things at a more cautious pace than Becky and Brett but she didn't think her feelings for him were any less than Becky's were for Brett.

"How did it go when Brett first met your parents?" she asked. She was still feeling hugely nervous about her own family dinner on Thursday.

225

"It was great. They got on really well, my mum and dad really liked him," Becky said.

"They weren't worried about you moving over to stay with him so soon?"

"No, my dad always wanted me to travel and I've still got the choice of coming back here if I don't like it over there."

Becky meant if she and Brett didn't work out, but of course didn't want to put that into words. "But what about you and Stewart? He's asked you over there too hasn't he?"

Not like Brett had asked Becky. It was a much more casual proposition. "Sort of."

"It'll be so great, all of us meeting up over there. Christmas on the beach too!"

Alice ended up hanging round with Becky for most of the evening as the two of them weren't on the pull. Jules was having a wild night, flirting with everyone in sight. Alice eventually saw her locked into an embrace with Mike Jackson on the dance floor.

"I didn't see that coming," she said to Becky.

"Me neither. He's not bad looking though is he? Honestly though she's had so much to drink she probably doesn't know what she's doing."

Alice wondered. Thinking back, she could remember Jules admiring Mike in the past. And she had even encouraged Alice to go for it with Joe Jackson. Maybe she had been hiding a secret crush?

She saw Maddy Pullen a couple of times, but Maddy carefully avoided them. Amazing to think that with all their lengthy and bitter history with her, she'd finally met her match in Becky.

* * *

Feeling extravagant Alice grabbed a taxi to Stewart's place. The night air was freezing compared to the thick, hot atmosphere of the nightclub and she was glad of her jacket even though it was summer. A couple of years ago the three of them used to suffer and freeze to save a quid on the cloakroom fee, but thanks to earnings from her vet job Alice could splash out on a ticket these days.

She felt strange going up to his flat by herself. But once she was inside it was just amazing to be with him again. In private, just the two of them.

His reaction to her outfit was also what she'd hoped for. She had deliberately chosen one of her shortest, most closely fitting dresses that she'd bought for a dare on a shopping trip some time ago.

It had won admiring glances in the nightclub but she was only interested in his response.

"Is that what I've been missing all night?" His gaze was thick with lust.

"All yours now." She smiled as she stood before him. The dress had a zip all the way down the back and she wanted him to open it and feel his hands down her spine.

"I was going to offer you coffee but that can wait." He came over to her, and instead of putting his arms around her body straight away, he cupped her face in his hands and kissed her. He was surprisingly tender. She was expecting him to crush her against him and ravish her.

But he stroked her hair and ran his hands down her shoulders and arms. She wanted to be pressed against him but he was standing back from her. Then he kissed her shoulder, moving across to her collarbone and the sensitive hollows by her neck. She shivered.

At the same time she felt his hands tug on her zip, and draw it down slowly. So slowly. He turned her around so her back faced him, and he pushed her dress apart and let it fall to the ground.

Still he didn't run his hands all over her. Instead he kissed her down her spine, from her neck to the curve of her lower back, unclasping her bra and pushing it off her.

He turned her back to face him and his fingers slipped beneath the sides of her underwear and drew it down over her hips, letting it slip to the floor as well.

She was now entirely naked in front of him. She had been naked with him before but not quite like this. He was gazing at her, drinking her whole body in with his eyes.

She felt oddly vulnerable but also cherished. Worshipped.

He seemed more silent than usual. The air between them held tension: it was sexual, but there was something else. Alice felt he wanted something from her but she wasn't sure what it was. She longed to touch him, so she reached for him and he helped push his own clothes off when she went to unbutton his shirt.

Now they faced one another, both naked. Once again she marvelled at his body: the athleticism of it, the masculine definition. And his hardness. He was so hard and ready for her.

She lifted her arms up to draw him down to kiss her, but he scooped her up and carried her onto the bed. He kissed her from her mouth to her breasts to her stomach and lower still. Finally he was touching her properly and she was moaning with relief at the feel of his hands on her body, while hers explored his.

His head was between her legs, suckling her. Somehow he had discovered exactly what worked for her: what place, what pressure, what rhythm. She was helpless beneath him.

Just as she was about to go over the edge, which he must have known from her gasps and the movements of her body against him, he stopped and broke away.

He drew himself up over her and looked into her eyes.

As ever she was mesmerised by his chiselled looks and how she felt about him. How he made her feel in both her body and her mind.

For a moment he was still. Intense. Grey blue eyes burning into her own. He brushed a strand of hair back from her face.

"I love you, Alice."

As he spoke he moved her legs apart and drove into her. The shock of what he had said and the sensation of him inside her made her cry out. Suddenly she found herself climaxing, spasming in intense, helpless waves as his mouth came down on her own, kissed her cheek, her neck.

Just as the waves were ebbing into a warm, dizzy glow she felt him come too, pressing into her as hard and close as possible, grinding the two of them together as one person.

Alice was half sobbing, she was so overwhelmed. "I love you too. So much."

She couldn't see his face because it was buried in her neck but he held her even more tightly to him. He didn't leave her body even though he was fully spent. She clung to him in return, exhausted, ecstatic.

* * *

Alice must have fallen asleep immediately. She didn't remember anything else until she woke to find him draped over her, still unconscious himself.

There was a faint grey light seeping around the edge of the blind. It must be dawn.

She remembered what he had said last night. Had he meant it? Did he really love her, or was he just carried away by the moment?

She tried to close her eyes and fall asleep again but he stirred and she opened her eyes once more to see him looking at her. She couldn't read the expression on his face but it was as though he was studying her.

He bent his head to kiss her good morning. She snuggled happily against him.

"Last night, what you said, did you… I mean did you mean it?"

"Do I love you? Of course I do, I wouldn't have got into this if I didn't feel this way about you."

She felt her stomach flip. He actually loved her. Stewart Walker loved her.

"It's ok if you aren't sure though," he said. "If you're not ready, or you don't feel the same, it's no problem."

"I do feel the same. Very much."

He caressed her body, running his hand over her breast and down her stomach. "You are so beautiful, Alice. I didn't expect anything like this to happen. I certainly wasn't planning on it."

"When did you first feel it? Or know that you did?" She wanted to hear everything, every detail.

He traced his finger around her nipple, making her writhe in pleasure. "Very early on, looking back. But I first knew for certain at that party in Gloucester. I've never felt more violent than when I saw that brute attacking you. My girl. I might have killed him if Chris hadn't pulled me off him."

His girl. She was his.

"I was giving up on you ever making a move. I felt like I was flinging myself at you all the time and you weren't interested," she said.

"You have no idea. Stopping myself that first time in the pavilion was one of the hardest feats of my life."

"You were so angry that day." Alice remembered the way he had bruised her lip, and how much it had made her crave him even more.

"Because I wanted you so badly," he told her. "And I thought you were messing me around."

"I probably wanted it even more than you did."

"More than now?"

He moved her hand onto him, where he was already thick and hard beyond belief.

"Maybe about that much," she said, smiling.

"Good, because I have no plans to stop this time."

He rolled on top of her and showed her just how little he planned to hold back.

29. Dinner

The doorbell rang. Alice summoned up her courage. "I'll get it."

She knew it was Stewart, arriving at the perfect time for dinner. But she wanted to get a few moments with him before he was exposed to the ordeal of her family.

It wasn't that she was ashamed of her parents but more that Stewart was in such a different sphere of her life. His coming to dinner felt like inviting Richard to a nightclub.

He looked incredibly handsome when she opened the door. He bent to kiss her and she wished it could be just the two of them, doing their own thing, without the ordeal that lay ahead.

Bracing herself for her parents' reaction, particularly her mother's, she led him into the living room. Richard and her mother were still in the kitchen so it was just her brothers with their toys scattered all over the floor.

"They'll be in bed soon," she said, feeling a need to apologise for their presence.

"Do you drive a fire-engine?" the eldest one asked him and before Alice could hush them away they were plying him with vehicles and drawing him into their game. He had a way with people, she thought. Half the boys at school hero worshipped him - he was a good coach, admittedly - so perhaps it was no surprise that her brothers were drawn to him.

She watched how he played with them. He seemed to find it easy and didn't shrug them off like other visitors often did. Alice couldn't remember if he'd said he had nephews or nieces but he was obviously used to kids.

Richard entered the room and Stewart got up to shake his hand and give him the bottle of wine he had brought. He was taller than Richard and broader built, but Richard still looked very presentable, even stately. Alice felt weirdly proud of them both.

She was racked with nerves over what Richard would think of him. But Richard was civil with everyone, always flawlessly polite and well-mannered. She would have to wait until afterwards for his verdict because it was impossible to discern from his reaction. She thought he seemed genuinely favourable towards Stewart.

"He drives a fire-engine," her brother told Richard by way of introduction and Stewart laughed. Alice had no idea where her brother had got the idea that he was a fireman but it didn't seem to bother him.

Her mother entered, apologising for not greeting him earlier, as she had been held up in the kitchen. Alice suspected the delay was deliberate, and that her mother had wanted Richard to make his own assessment first.

Her mother's reaction was more interesting. She flushed slightly when Stewart shook her hand. She was less at ease than Richard but that was to be expected. No one was ever as unruffled and inscrutable as Richard.

She doesn't hate him on sight anyway, Alice thought. It was pretty impossible not to be impressed by Stewart physically: he was so incredibly good looking and his clothes always sat perfectly on him. He was smartly dressed but not overly formal. Just right. Her mother wouldn't be able to find fault there anyway.

The conversation had sprung up around the usual sort of small talk about how long Stewart had been in England, and whether it was his first visit, and what his impressions were. Alice was torn between wanting to escape for a few minutes and put the boys to bed, and not leaving the three of them alone without her. She found herself tongue-tied. It felt like her parents and Stewart were the grown-ups and she was one of the kids with her brothers.

Stewart brought her into the conversation with ease, turning the subject to her own travels.

"They've been planning it for a while, Alice and her friend Jules," her mother told him. "I get anxious, of course, about them travelling so far but they're both quite sensible girls."

Alice literally wanted to sink through the floor with embarrassment. She felt like she was being discussed in front of an elderly aunt. The only thing that could make this worse would be if her mother and Richard started referring to "young people".

In the end Richard took the boys off to bed and when he returned they all went through to the dining room. It looked nice at least, her mother had put flowers on the table which suggested she was making an effort to be welcoming.

Dinner went far more smoothly than Alice had dared hope. She still didn't manage to say very much initially, but the conversation kept going and Richard and Stewart actually seemed to find various topics of common ground. World events, history, even sport.

It fact it all went very well. There was no awkwardness between the three of them, however Alice herself might be feeling. Stewart and Richard continued to draw her into the conversation and it ended up being a very pleasant meal.

Difficult subjects, such as how Alice and Stewart had met, were never raised. Alice went from being in a state of high nervous tension to actually enjoying herself. She could tell that both Richard and her mother liked Stewart. Whether they approved of her going out with him was a different matter but she'd passed the first hurdle.

Afterwards Alice walked him out to his car. "Your parents are great," he said.

"I think they liked you."

He laughed. "No shotguns anyway. I'll see you tomorrow night? Will you stay over?"

"If you want me to." She wanted more of an invitation.

"I want you to more than anything else in this world. I want you tonight, right now, but I know that's not possible." To prove it he kissed her, pressing her against him, and she could feel his need for her.

They were ok. Her and Stewart. He still wanted her, still loved her, she hoped. The ordeal of meeting her parents hadn't sent him running for the hills.

* * *

After she had helped her parents clear up the dinner table and stack the dishwasher, Alice went to her mother's room while she got ready for bed. Richard had tactfully taken himself off to his study to look at a letter or something.

"So?" Alice couldn't wait any longer for the official verdict.

"I think he's a very nice man. Incredibly good looking, not that that should matter of course. Exactly the kind of man I would be very happy for you to date."

"But?" She could hear there was a but.

Her mother sighed. She put down the necklace she had just taken off and looked at Alice.

"I wonder if you're being fair to him, darling."

This was a shock. Alice had expected any censure to fall on Stewart, not her.

"What do you mean?"

"You have to consider where he is in life. Of course he's older than you, but it's more than that. You're at such different life stages. You're about to go travelling, Alice, then to university. You'll be meeting any number of new young people, young men. He's clearly in love with you and it won't be easy for him when you move on."

"I don't intend to move on," Alice said. "I love him as well." She was very happy that her mother thought that Stewart loved her. Somehow it gave it more validity for her mother to have noticed.

"But think about what his wants and expectations are. At his stage of life he probably wants to settle down and have a family. You're nowhere near ready for that."

Alice couldn't refute this point. "Not now, maybe. But one day."

"My fear is that he will wait for you, and put his life on hold, and you'll either change your mind or feel trapped in something that you no longer want."

The problem was that her mother made sense. Frustratingly. Alice couldn't deny her reasoning. But she also knew how she felt about Stewart. Of course she wanted to travel and study veterinary science. Yet if he asked her to go to the ends of the earth with him instead, she would do so. And she probably wouldn't mind, though she knew that he would never ask her that.

Still, her mother had made her uneasy. Alice was sure she knew her own heart, but what if her mother was right? People did fall in and out of love.

And what if he fell out of love with her? The thought that he might go back to Australia and forget about her was almost too much to bear.

"Do you really think he's that serious about me?" she asked. She wasn't sure whether she wanted reassurance that he was or that he wasn't.

"Think about what he's risked to be with you, Alice. His job, his reputation. And then he came here and met us. People don't do that if their feelings are only casual, not men like him anyway. He would have made an excuse and avoided us."

It was almost exactly what Jules had said to her just a couple of weeks ago. Alice had been briefly unsettled then and was more so now. Was she leading him on? Was she denying him the chance to meet someone and settle down and raise a family in the near future?

When she'd been pursuing him for all those weeks she had never thought about the long-term, it was all in the moment. "Do you want me to stop seeing him?" she asked.

"It's not what I want, Alice, or even what I think is best. I'm just worried for both of you that you haven't really thought about the consequences of this. Enjoy yourself with him this summer if it continues, but just be careful not to get yourself into any commitments that you can't keep. Be fair to him and to yourself."

Lying in her bed that night Alice couldn't sleep for hours as her mother's words had left her so conflicted. Did she love him enough? She was sure she did. Just the thought of him made her stomach flip and her body long to be in his arms. She liked him. She enjoyed being with him, they laughed at the same things.

A small secret part of her already wanted him to think of her in a long-term way. She wanted to be his. But now she was scared she couldn't trust her own constancy. Was she a fickle person? Was she being unfair to him?

She wished Becky and Jules were there so she could talk it over with them. She was seeing them both tomorrow - Becky had persuaded them to watch the cricket again as Gloucestershire were playing at home - so she could share her anxieties then.

30. Doubt

"Maddy Pullen was right you know," Jules said as they sat watching the afternoon's play in the half-empty stands of the County Ground in Bristol.

"About what?"

"We have turned into cricket groupies. Every one of us is dating a cricketer." Jules was seeing Mike Jackson again later that evening.

Alice felt a bit of a fraud because she still didn't find the game very interesting and wished she could have brought a book to read.

She suspected that Becky didn't enjoy it much either, but kept quiet out of loyalty to Brett. Or maybe it was different when you were actually watching your own boyfriend play.

"I'm not with Brett because he's a cricketer though," Becky said.

"I didn't say you were."

"We're not groupies then, it's just coincidence."

Cricketers who were all at very different stages of their careers, Alice thought. Mike who was still playing schoolboy cricket, Brett who was playing professionally, and Stewart who had retired. Even though it had been early and possibly temporary, due to injury, it still reminded her of what her mother had said.

There was a subdued cheer as Gloucestershire took another wicket.

"Honestly you wonder how they're even motivated to play on weekdays. There's hardly anyone here," Jules said. Looking around the stands, the majority of spectators appeared to be elderly men. There were a few businessmen who had possibly bunked off work early but it was hardly a lively crowd.

The others had noticed Alice was quieter than usual. "Everything alright with you and Stewie?" Jules asked.

"Yes. He came round for dinner last night."

"Oh god. I forgot about that. What was it like? Did your parents freak?"

"No, it went really well," Alice told her.

"Why are you so down then? School's out, you're not getting locked up in your bedroom, you should be on top of the world." Jules was already on top of the world again. She had recovered from her heartbreak over Leafy with lightning speed and was fully enjoying the summer holidays and months of freedom.

"It's just something my mother said." She told them about the conversation.

"He hasn't asked you about any of that though, has he? Marriage and kids and stuff?" Becky asked.

"No. Has Brett asked you?"

"We've talked about it, but only in the sense that we both want to wait a few years, whatever happens. He wants to play for Australia, I want to graduate. There's no rush."

Alice envied how easy things must be for Becky, being so much closer in age to Brett.

"He's not that old you know, really," Jules said. "I mean how old was Richard when he had your brothers? Practically fifty probably."

Alice supposed this was so.

"Anyway let's face it," Jules continued. "You've only been seeing him for a couple of months. Weeks really, given how hesitant he was. It's a bit premature to be worrying about this."

Jules was right, but Alice still felt odd about things. She was seeing Stewart later that evening and now almost wished she wasn't so she could have more time to think about things.

After play finished that afternoon Becky was going to stay down in Bristol with Brett, and Jules and Alice were driving back to Cheltenham. "You've got time for a drink in the bar first haven't you?" Becky asked them.

They agreed to go in for one drink. The usual crowd soon gathered: Chris, Brett, Grant, Graeme and a couple of others. "The Headmaster not with you?" Grant asked.

"No, she's got detention later," Jules told him. There was the usual ribbing, but Alice got the sense that no one actually disapproved. Everyone accepted her being with Stewart just as they accepted Becky and Brett.

Chris in particular seemed pleased they'd finally got together. "You've been good for him."

"Have I?"

"He had put a bit of a wall up, after what happened. He's been wary," Chris told her.

"Did he tell you we got caught?" Alice asked.

Chris laughed. "Yeah. Surprised they didn't sack him."

"You and the Headmaster got caught up to no good?" Graeme asked, overhearing.

Alice explained what had had happened with them being seen together at a restaurant.

"That's hardly incriminating. I was expecting something X-rated in the school pavilion," Graeme said.

Alice had to stand on Jules' foot to stop her blurting anything out. Unfortunately Graeme picked up on this and what did or didn't happen in the pavilion became the joke for the rest of the hour.

* * *

"You really should talk to him about it," Jules said as they headed back up the motorway to Cheltenham.

Alice couldn't imagine how she could start such a conversation. Particularly when everything should be going perfectly right now. They were finally together, publicly, no obstacles.

"You're seeing him tonight, aren't you?" Jules continued. "Just let him know that you don't want to make any life decisions before you graduate."

It sounded simple but really it wasn't. Alice looked out of the window at the countryside rushing past them. It was such a perfect day. Nothing could ever feel better than the start of summer: even if it turned wet and miserable later in July, it was how it started that set the tone for the entire season.

The freedom ahead of them was exhilarating, overwhelming. Was that why she was suddenly feeling panicked? Because there were no boundaries any more, no rules? Nothing to control any of them except their own choices and decisions.

Wanting to change the subject because there was no point dwelling on it she asked Jules about her date with Mike Jackson.

"It's nothing serious," Jules said. "It's just, you know, lust."

Alice did know. The thought of it, the thought of the whole night that lay ahead with Stewart, suffused her with it. They were supposed to be going out on the town first but she wondered if she could persuade him to stay in and spend the entire evening in bed instead.

Somehow being alone with him seemed less confronting than being around other people. It was more of a bubble. She could shut out the rest of the world and reality. Besides, the thought of hours being naked together, just the two of them, was a delight in itself.

"You're obviously thinking of your coach, you have that infuriating smile on your face again," Jules said.

"I was actually thinking of our travels."

Jules laughed. "Liar."

If Jules could read her like a book would she be able to hide her doubts from Stewart? With what she felt was a steely resolve Alice attempted to suppress them, determined to enjoy herself and not waste a single hour she got to spend with him. God knows she had wanted this so much, for so long.

"There's probably going to be a festival next weekend down in Devon, somewhere called Smeathorpe. I'm thinking of going," Jules said.

"What if Leafy's there? You might bump into him."

"That's the point. Then he'll see I don't care."

Which meant Jules probably did still care, Alice thought. "What about Mike?" she asked.

"I'm going to be a cricket widow that weekend anyway, he's playing club cricket. I'm turning into Becky," Jules said.

* * *

Alice chose another short and hopefully seductive dress that evening, and from the reaction in Stewart's eyes when he came to pick her up she had made the right choice for her plans.

As he drove off she put her hand on his thigh and moved it up, causing him to start. "You'll make me crash," he warned.

Moving her hand higher she felt how he was already hard for her. "That's going to be awkward in the Dog & Duck, isn't it?"

"If you keep doing that, it is."

She looked at his profile; he was trying to stay fixed on the road. "Why don't we just go back to your place?"

"What's brought this on? Can't you wait for it?" he asked. He was smiling now, glancing at her as he drove.

"Can you?"

"Not easily, with you wearing that."

"Drive faster then," she ordered.

When they got to his place they practically ran up the steps. Inside he grabbed her and pulled her to him. She didn't resist. It was raw, passionate and urgent. A mutual need.

She found herself clawing at his back to bring him closer into her, begging him for more, faster, harder.

He was in charge, pulling her whichever way he wanted, screwing her from the side, behind, on top, underneath. Even in some positions when he was almost thrusting too deep, almost hurting her it was ok. She still wanted more, deeper. She was insatiable.

And he couldn't get enough of her, he had never been so forceful and so demanding. Even when he had taken her over the sofa after the cinema was nothing compared to this.

"God I love you," he cried out just before he came. "You're perfect, you're mine and you're perfect."

It brought her over with him, she was calling out his name and her need for him.

They lay there together for some time, limbs tangled, slick and exhausted.

He restarted by trailing his hand over her nipples and down between her legs. His touch was like electricity to her. All her nerves responded. Even though she was almost sore from the intensity of what he had just been doing to her, she still gasped as he flicked a finger over her most sensitive button.

But this time he was slower, gentler, playing with her. He ran a finger around her entrance and then inside her. Compared to how he had filled her before it was nothing, but then he slipped a second finger in. Reaching in deeper, his other hand playing with her nipple he curled his fingers inside her.

The pressure was strange but nice. He was twisting them, stretching her a little. She could feel sensitive waves throbbing from deep inside her, much more internal than usual, making her writhe on his hand.

She wanted his thumb against her nub again, she would have orgasmed instantly if he touched her there, but he only focused on inside her.

He wanted her to come for him like this, deeply, with her whole body at his mercy.

She felt his fingers move and push and twist, and then she realised he had added a third. The added stretch intensified the feeling inside, as he pressed against her sensitive walls. Now she was lying back, her eyes closed, helpless at his touch. Making faint cries she could barely control.

"Don't stop, never stop."

It felt like he went for ages, holding her on the edge, not quite letting her fall over it but stopping her from climbing down. It was a kind of torture. She wanted release but there was this endless build up instead, she wasn't sure how much more she could take.

"I need..."

He knew what she needed but he was going to make her wait, to draw it out. His hand was clasping her breast and his mouth went down on her nipple, his tongue swirling around as he sucked her.

It sent a pang through her but still not enough, not enough...

Now she was begging him. Asking him please, moving and shifting around to intensify the feeling of his fingers inside her.

And finally he let her over the edge. He bent his fingers further within her, hooking them against her, adding pressure to a hyper sensitive place she hadn't even known existed. He was fully in control. Her body was literally his to play with, to command.

Half sobbing she felt strange, deep waves ripped through her. Her body was actually shaking. She was saying his name over and over. Her head felt dizzy and she actually passed out.

When she came round, probably just moments later, he cradled her to him. And gently, because her whole body was too dizzy for her to be able to do much, he entered her again and rocked into her.

It was tender and sweet and close. His lips were on hers and she was drowning into him. He was rock hard but he still took his time, drawing it out for his own pleasure now.

Alice thought she must be absolutely drained of the ability to orgasm again, ever perhaps, but his gentle thrusts began to awaken her body again. She wasn't sure how long they lay like this, joined, coupled, with him stroking into her in such small movements, but it could have been an hour or more.

Slowly, surely it built up again and as he came inside her she reached the peak for a third time. And then she knew nothing, for they both slept.

31. Uncertainty

Later in the night, though still before midnight, Alice woke and felt her guilty misgivings return. Stewart lay there, satisfied and dozing, his arm lying across her stomach. It made her think what he might want from her, sooner than she was ready, and she felt panicked.

She twisted away and sat on the edge of the bed. He remained asleep and she didn't want to wake him. But he was roused nonetheless.

"Something's up, isn't it? What's the matter?" he asked.

"Nothing, I'm fine."

But he wasn't going to be fooled that easily. "Is something worrying you?"

"No." She hoped the lie didn't make her voice sound hollow.

Stewart stroked the hair back from her face.

Suddenly she burst into tears, hating herself for it, feeling like an idiotic child. But she still couldn't tell him, it would only make it worse.

He put his arms around her and she wept into his chest. It was where Alice wanted to be but she couldn't quell her thoughts and fears nor communicate them to him. She felt that she was leading him on, even though she wanted to be with more than anything else in the world.

He searched around for ideas. "Do you want me to drive you home?" At first she thought he was rejecting her but then she saw the love and concern in his eyes and it made her want to cry even more.

She didn't want to leave him but she also wanted to clear her head. She had thought that being with him would blot out her doubts but she felt guilty the more kindness he showed her.

"I'm sorry," she said, managing to recover. "I didn't mean to be a downer."

He put his arms around her. "If you're worried about anything, you can tell me. We'll fix it together."

But she couldn't tell him. Together might be the whole problem.

"I'm fine, I really am. I'm sorry for waking you." She lay back down with him and he held her in his arms. He soon fell asleep again but Alice lay awake for what felt like hours.

She was torn. Torn in terms of wanting to be with him but fear that she was being selfish in doing so.

* * *

The worst thing was that she wouldn't see him for all the next week. Stewart had to take the Fairmount cricket team to a five-day tournament across the country. And now she had made a complete mess of their last night together.

The morning had still been uncomfortable and Alice was frustrated with herself. She should be totally happy, he hadn't made any demands on her after all, but the fear that he might have different expectations to her continued to ring in her head. She tried to act normally but he could tell something was still up.

He drove her home, and when he kissed her goodbye she felt herself melting into him all over again. Even though it was broad daylight she wanted to make love with him then and there, in the car, Hilary Bowes' twitching curtains be damned. She wanted to give him something to remember her by, other than her being a basket case the previous night.

She started trying to unbutton his shirt, wanting to run her hands over the muscles of his chest.

"Do you want me to drive somewhere more discreet?"

Alice directed him to a dead-end lane a short drive away, a popular place for parked cars with steamed up windows on weekend nights. On Saturday morning there were only a couple of empty cars there, probably people walking their dogs in the fields beyond.

He parked the car and leaned over to her to kiss her again. But she pushed him over to his side and sat on top of him, straddling him. She loved feeling the hardness of him through his clothes, all for her.

So she unbuckled his belt, opening his fly and tugging it apart. His erection sprang up into her hands almost instantly, freed from the restrictions of clothing. As she brought her mouth down on him he caught his breath and a part of her rejoiced that she could have such an effect on him.

"If someone walks past..." his breathing was ragged. But he wasn't going to stop her.

She could feel his own desire, pent up again even though it wasn't that long since the last time.

He didn't let her continue for long before he pulled her up and against his chest. He pushed her underwear aside and was quickly inside her. Hot, hard, tight.

In this position he could easily touch any part of her body, through her clothes and under her clothes, rub her against his fingers. And he did so. He drove her wild.

They were face to face, looking into one another's eyes. She read love there, desire. She wanted him so much that any good resolutions she had to be sensible or to be patient simply evaporated.

She was grinding onto him, loving the depth, the connection. He pulled her close against him and she clung to him, her face against the side of his neck, breathing in his scent to try and store it in her mind for the time they would be apart.

"How am I going to manage for a week without this?" he asked her as he gripped her hips with his hands, working her to his rhythm. Then the light in his eyes softened. "Without you?"

Alice didn't know how she was going to manage either which was absurd since she'd coped just fine without him or anyone else before.

But she was hooked now. They both were. She wanted to be with him all the time. She just needed it to be in the moment, not thinking too far ahead.

"Will you be thinking of me?" she asked.

"All week. Dreaming about you as well, I should think."

"What kind of dreams?"

"You know what kind," he told her.

"Will I do this?" She twisted on him and squeezed, knowing that if she kept it up she could easily make him lose control.

"You will now."

"Will you forget what I look like?" She was obviously teasing him now as she lifted her top, exposing her body to him. His hands went straight to her breasts, fondling them and making her whole body tingle with pleasure.

"I think this image should stick in my mind."

The extra stimulation as his thumbs brushed her nipples was bringing her close to the peak, and as he shifted beneath her suddenly, driving in deeper, she lost it just ahead of him.

He held her for a while afterwards. They talked, half serious, half joking, about how much he would miss her during the week.

"If you had a phone in your bedroom I could call you up at night," he said.

"I could use the hall phone. No one would hear if they were all asleep." Though the ringing might wake them, she supposed.

"You'd need to be in bed for what I'd want to tell you to do."

Alice shivered at the thought. She'd heard of people having phone sex but never tried anything like it herself. The prospect of Richard or her mother picking up one of the extensions was dreadful. Plus the ringing might wake everyone up.

"I'll see what I can do." The hall phone might just reach into her bedroom, if she threaded it through the bannisters. What her parents would think was quite another matter. Perhaps if she put a blanket over the phone it might muffle the ring and not wake them.

Just thinking about it was starting to turn her on again, and she started wondering if he would have recovered enough stamina yet.

Then she saw someone walking along the lane towards the car. She had totally forgotten where they were and the fact that anyone could see in. Quickly she pulled her top down and dived back onto her seat, hoping the morning dog-walker wouldn't notice anything unusual.

Stewart grinned. "You don't want to give him a show?"

"No. And it's a she, anyway." The mortifying thought that it might even be someone she knew was enough to bring Alice back down to earth.

He drove her back home, he was already running late due to their diversion so couldn't come in for a drink. Parting from him felt harder than it ever had before. What on earth was it going to be like when she had to go overseas and he had to go back to Australia? She decided to avoid thinking about it as much as possible.

"So you'll call me?"

"Of course. I don't want you getting bored and finding other diversions." He was joking but she sensed the same, slight insecurity in him that she felt herself. He was still not completely sure of her feelings for him. Her emotional outburst last night wouldn't have helped. And although he never said anything, she knew he was conscious of other guys like Joe Jackson hanging around the sidelines.

Not that he had anything to worry about. What terrified her was how completely and absolutely she wanted him and no one else. But he was her first, and she knew nothing else. He of course did, and in the moments when she wasn't fretting that she was leading him on and getting in too deep, she worried that she might not match up to the women in his past.

Was love always like this? Did something so wonderful also have to be so tricky and so nerve-wracking?

32. Separation

Alice was lingering around Richard's study once again, not really sure what she wanted to ask him or even if she wanted to ask him anything at all. She couldn't ask her mother for reassurance, because it was her mother's view that had disrupted her peace of mind in the first place.

"You did like Stewart, didn't you?" she said at last.

"I found him to be a very decent and intelligent man." Decent and intelligent. From Richard this was high praise.

"Do you think I'm too young? That it's a mistake?"

Richard didn't answer immediately, and Alice could see he was thinking.

"Certainly not a mistake, because no experience in life is a mistake," he said. "As for your age, you are both consenting adults. It's perhaps more an issue of timing."

"Timing?"

"The stages of where you both are in your lives. You're due to travel the world. He's going through a time of career transition. You know that significant changes lie ahead for you both, which is challenging."

He understood. Somehow, he always understood, and he never judged.

"If I keep seeing him, and it gets more serious, will it just make it harder?" Alice asked.

Once again Richard paused for thought. "I should think it would make it easier. At least you'll have a more definite picture of what you both want."

"But then we have to go our separate ways."

"That's not a difficult thing. Painful, perhaps. A more difficult situation would be confusion or uncertainty about what you wanted to do."

Alice looked at all the books lining the shelves of the room. Easily a lifetime's reading.

"What if I change my mind?"

"The sky won't fall if you do."

It felt better hearing this from Richard as a man. If he thought it was something that could be taken on the chin, perhaps Alice was worrying unduly.

* * *

During the next few days Alice tried to take her mind off things by throwing herself into work. She didn't want to be one of those girls that sat waiting by the telephone. Still, she wished he would ring. Every time the phone went her heart leapt and then she would kick herself for feeling disappointed when it turned out to be one of her mother's friends.

Jules was less than impressed when Alice answered her call with an "oh, it's you."

"I suppose that tone means you were hoping for your coach to ring. Hasn't he called you yet?" she asked.

"No. It's stupid but I keep stressing he's changed his mind."

"Hardly. Weren't you the one who was worried about him liking you more than you liked him, only last week?" Jules said.

That hadn't been quite Alice's concern, though if she had ever doubted her own feelings, the separation had been enough to assuage any concerns. She burned for him. Cheltenham felt bleak and empty without him there.

"It's only been four days, Alice, how on earth are you going to manage when we go travelling?"

Five days. It was Saturday when she had last seen and spoken with him, and it was now Thursday without word. Each day became a little more agonising.

"How are you going to manage without your cricket captain beau?" Alice asked.

Jules and Mike Jackson were surprisingly still infatuated though Jules swore it was just lust. Mike was also away on the tournament with Stewart so she was a fellow cricket widow that week.

"Let's go and drown our sorrows at the Dog & Duck." Jules had started doing some bartending shifts there which meant they could now get the occasional free drink.

Alice thought it might add to her sorrows, being the place she had first properly met Stewart, but she agreed to go. Anything was better than another night of sitting by the phone.

They didn't stay out late as Alice had to get up the next morning to work at the veterinary surgery, so she was back home by around half past ten. For the past few nights she had been taking the hall phone into her bedroom, with the aid of an extension cord she had found in a drawer, and putting it under a blanket to muffle it in case it rang.

Of course it would be this night, after she'd had too many drinks and needed to get an early night, that he finally called.

Alice practically leapt across the room to silence the phone. Even underneath several layers of blanket it sounded like a million decibels at this late hour. She hoped her mother and Richard hadn't heard. Their room was some distance away, insulated from hers by the bathroom and the boys' room, so hopefully not.

"Hello?" She hadn't even considered the possibility that it might not be him. But it was, and just hearing his voice made her flood with joy.

Stewart apologised for not having called earlier. "There's only a broken payphone where we're staying. I finally managed to get to a phone box in town, I'm sorry to call so late. I've missed you."

She had missed him too. She told him so.

"Where are you now?" he asked.

"I'm in my room, I was out with Jules earlier but I've got work tomorrow."

"You're alone?"

Of course she was. But she realised why he was asking.

"Yes, everyone else is asleep," she told him.

He was silent for a moment and she could almost feel him there in the room with her.

"I wish I was with you," he said.

She nearly cracked a joke from nerves, about her parents not appreciating a midnight visitor, but instead she said "I wish you were too."

"You know what I'd be doing to you right now?"

Even this far away from him, she shivered. She was clinging to the phone handset, holding it as close as possible to her ear as though that could somehow bring him nearer.

"What would you be doing?" She had a feeling he was going to tell her, so she slipped back into her bed, cradling the phone between her ear and the pillow.

"I'd have you naked with me. And I wouldn't be letting you sleep."

The thought of it made her throb for him. She wondered if he was also turned on. He must be standing in a phone box somewhere, in the dark. She hoped the coins wouldn't suddenly run out.

But she couldn't answer him. She felt shy, even though he couldn't see her face.

"Do you want me, Alice? Right now?"

Of course she did. "Yes, I really do."

"Touch yourself."

She didn't dare disobey. She was gripping the phone with one hand for dear life. She let her other hand slide down beneath her clothing and felt how incredibly wet she was for him, even with him being so far away.

"How does that feel?"

"I wish it was you doing it to me."

"I will be, soon. But right now I want you to imagine it's me."

He instructed her how to move her hand and where. The speed, the pressure.

She complied. She was so wet, so turned on. She couldn't speak, she could barely breathe. She was half panting, half gasping over the phone as she followed his commands.

He continued to tell her exactly what to do. His voice grew huskier as he issued each direction.

She grew wetter, more swollen, more sensitive.

"Now I want you to come for me."

She was in his hands. Even though he wasn't there. He was guiding her, step by step. She followed everything he told her to do.

"Swirl your finger around. Right where I know you want it."

She had to muffle her own cries as she came, hoping no one would hear, longing for him to be there to plunge inside her and press her to him and give her the fullness of it. "I want you. So much. Why aren't you here?" She was breathless.

"I will be there, this weekend. And I want you for the whole of it. You're going to stay with me and show me exactly what you did tonight."

"A repeat performance?" It had been hard enough doing it on the phone with him, she couldn't imagine doing it in front of him. In person, with him watching her.

But the thickness of desire in his voice told her how much he wanted it. Wanted her.

"I love you, Alice. Sleep well. I'll pick you up on Saturday night at eight. We should be back by then."

She couldn't sleep though. He had made her orgasm, but it fanned the fire rather than quenched it. She lay there, needing him again, needing him more. Just thinking about what he had said to her and made her do triggered all her desire again.

Plus the thought of what he might have in store for her that weekend. If she felt this desperate for him after only a few days absence she could only imagine what he might be feeling. And tonight had been all about her.

She couldn't believe how late it was when she looked at her bedside clock. Had they really been on the phone that long? Thank god he had called her, or she would have had some awkward explaining to do when the phone bill came with such a lengthy, late-night, long-distance call.

33. Resolution

Alice was ecstatic to see Stewart again when he picked her up on Saturday evening. But she was nervous too. The intensity of how she felt scared her.

He looked more tanned, having been out in the sun all week at the tournament.

"Did it go well?" she asked him.

"If you mean did we win, then yes," he told he.

"How did Mike do?" she asked, out of interest for Jules.

"Jackson? Two half centuries, I don't think he's going to have many worries with county selection."

Jules would be so happy for him, Alice thought. Even though she would probably pretend she wasn't bothered.

"So what are we doing tonight?"

"After eating boarding school food for a week, I need a decent meal," Stewart said. The tournament had been held in the grounds one of the schools taking part, and the teams and coaches had all been accommodated there.

They managed to find a restaurant that had a free table at that time on a Saturday night. He ordered steak and chips and Alice followed his lead. She wasn't actually that hungry, she'd been too wired all day with anticipation about seeing him again.

He asked her how her week had gone, and she told him about work. Someone had brought in what they claimed was a kitten to the surgery. Except it had actually turned out to be an ocelot, and given its owner had no licence and no idea about its proper care, Jo had had to call the RSPCA.

"They're restricted under the Dangerous Wild Animals Act. God only knows how he got hold of it, or why he took it to a regular vet," Alice said. "It was very sweet though. They're tiny, just like a regular domestic kitten. The leopard fur rather gives it away."

"Does that happen a lot?"

"Animals that exotic? No. Owners not having a clue how to care for something, all the time," she told him.

"It must be frustrating," Stewart said.

"It drives Jo mad. It's one of the reasons she's happy to be leaving for South Africa. There's only so much of that you can take, seeing animals not cared for properly and not always being able to do anything."

"What about you?"

"I think I'd like to work with exotics one day. If I specialised, I wouldn't really be dealing with everyday owners," Alice said. "I have to get into vet school first of course, and then actually pass everything."

"You'll be fine. You're easily smart enough."

She didn't know how he could be certain of this, but she loved that he had confidence in her. "What about you? Have you decided what you want to do when you go back to Australia?" It was a horrible thought, that he would be leaving to go so far away. At least she'd be leaving for her trip around the same time.

"I'll probably take some time and decide when I'm over there. There's no rush. There are jobs here as well."

"In England? You'd stay here?"

"Longer term it's definitely an option." He looked at her as he said this, and she felt a thrill in the pit of her stomach. Part happiness, part fear. For a fleeting moment she imagined going to veterinary school with him in travelling distance, rather than the other side of the world. Would he really do that for her? Was it wise to even hope for it?

* * *

Later they were at his place, and Alice had been continuing to flip between happiness and a strange sense of panic. On one hand she was thrilled by the thought of Stewart in her future. On the other hand she didn't feel ready to commit to anything yet.

She was worried, given what he had gone through to be with her and the risks he had taken, that maybe he would expect some kind of guarantee.

They were drinking coffee before going to bed and though she tried she was unable to hide her conflicting emotions.

Stewart discerned her anxiety.

"Something's been troubling you, hasn't it? You can tell me."

He was looking directly into her eyes and she saw love there and concern.

She bit the bullet. Took a deep breath. She was going to have to have this conversation eventually.

"I worry that I can't be what you want. Yet anyway. It's not that I don't love you, I just don't know yet if I can... make decisions." She knew she was garbling and sounding even more confused. She was also getting more confused in her own head.

"What do you think I want from you?" he asked her.

"It's just, with you having been married and everything. You're probably ready for different things and I can't do that or be that, yet anyway," Alice said.

Stewart was smiling. "So you think my plan is to set up a white picket fence with a couple of kids in the next twelve months, is that it?"

"No. Well, not exactly, it's just that you must have thought about those things when you were married, and maybe you might be ready for all that again, soon."

Now he was laughing. "I can't believe you've been worrying about that. I love you, but we have all the time in the world. There's no way I'd ever rush you or pressure you into something. If I wanted that - if I wanted it now with someone - I would never have made a move on you. It would have been unfair to both of us. But if we both feel the same way in a few years' time we can have a different conversation."

She was hugely relieved but also embarrassed for bringing it up.

"I'm sorry. I just panic from time to time. I haven't felt like this with anyone before."

He stroked her hair back off her face. "Nor have I. Not with Bree, not with anyone. It took meeting you to make me realise what it should be like. But I'm not on a timetable. When I say years, I mean years. I want you to graduate, figure out what you want to do and where you want to be. And if that's with someone else, then I'll deal with it."

"You might too," Alice said. "Fall for someone else, I mean."

He laughed again. "I doubt it. The one advantage I have being older is that I have enough experience to know how you compare. But I'm well aware that you don't. And if you need to find that out, then that's what you have to do."

Alice couldn't imagine this in a million years. Every other guy just seemed insubstantial compared to him. Just looking at him now she couldn't help wanting him. Thinking about the hard muscles under his clothes, the warmth of his skin, how his hands felt touching her all over her body.

"If you want me to compare you to other guys, you'd better start by showing me what you're capable of."

He looked surprised for a moment, then realised that she was teasing him. "You need reminding?"

"Yes, I've forgotten. Completely."

"Have you forgotten this?" He tilted her head back and kissed her lips, first gently then firmly, his tongue exploring her, entwining with hers. His hands cupped her backside and he moulded her against him so she could feel his heat and strength. She loved the height of him, how tall and powerful he was. "And this?" He ran his hands down her sides, his thumbs brushing her breasts through the thin cotton covering them, his mere touch causing her nipples to go taut.

"This too?" His lips were in the hollow of her neck now, his hands slid between her legs, caressing up her thigh and slipping inside the fabric of her underwear. She was already slick and ready for him. As always, he knew exactly where to touch her.

"I can't remember any of it." She could barely breathe the words, she was so hazy with desire for him.

"And this? You've forgotten this?" He had pulled her top open and had his mouth on her breast, his tongue swirling around her nipple just as his fingers probed her near her most sensitive place, not touching directly but just circling around, driving her crazy. She squirmed to get him to touch her there but he had no intention of giving her release that early.

Then he slipped a finger inside her and it made her want him inside her properly so badly she actually whimpered.

"Do you need me to show you exactly what I can do with you?" he asked.

"Yes." Please, she thought.

But he teased her mercilessly. Drawing everything out as long as possible, making her cling to him and beg him to fill her, to return to her.

"Don't stop!" she said for what felt like the hundredth time. He was deliberately working her up to the edge then drawing back, leaving her helpless.

"I need to make sure you remember this. If it's quick you might forget too easily." He was joking but he was also proving a point. She needed him desperately and he wanted her to realise that.

She clung to his back, trying to draw him closer to her, she wanted him deep and hard. But he was so much stronger than her that he maintained total control.

She was pleading with him to stop holding back. He was playing her body with absolute precision, touching her so nearly at the spot where she needed it, then ceasing and moving his hands elsewhere.

Her whole body was on fire for him. She was weak with need.

"I love you, I can't wait any longer." She was crying out for him.

At last, finally he entered her. Filling her, stretching her, sating her with his hardness.

They were joined. They were one. They were as physically close as it was possible to be.

Surely no one else could ever compare to this?

His hands were gripping her waist, his thumbs splayed over her lower stomach. He set the rhythm, the depth, the pace. He held her there. He was unrelenting.

He was showing her just how easily he could own her body. She could do nothing to resist him and she didn't want to do anything to resist him.

She wanted him. Only him.

He brought her to the peak just as he reached it, moving his hands up over her body and breasts, and lying over her, shifting his angle to bring them even tighter together.

His hard, final thrusts caused her insides to contract with sensation that was so intense it was almost painful. She was so out of breath she felt faint and light-headed.

* * *

Afterwards Alice should have been shattered but she felt awake and alive all over her body. Stars were dancing inside her head and inside the room.

Stewart lay beside her, also recovering. "Will that be easier to remember?"

She smiled. She felt enthralled by him, saturated by him and only him. This man, with his powerful body and his hands that knew how to make her body his. She looked at his face, the chiselled angles of his jaw, his even brow, his lips. She was memorising all of his features like a book.

"I can't imagine ever wanting anyone else like I want you," she told him.

She saw the light in his eyes when she said this but he still wasn't going to hold her to anything.

"What I want, Alice, is just to enjoy the next few months with you, if that's what you want too. No pressure. When you go travelling and when I go back to Australia, we can both see how we feel. If you want to come and visit me in Australia then we'll arrange it and take it from there."

It was exactly what she needed to hear. The fact he understood and was on the same page as her made it all feel even more right.

He brought his lips to hers and the dizzy joy of being with him - no more school, no more obstacles - flooded through her.

They had so much time. The summer had only just begun.

Epilogue

The slant seas leaning on the mangrove copse,
And summer basking in the sultry plains
About a land of canes;

The Progress of Spring, Alfred, Lord Tennyson

Brisbane, November 1992

Alice had been incredibly nervous on the flight from Bali to Australia. Not just about whether Stewart would still feel the same way, but how she would feel when she saw him.

It was only three months since they'd said goodbye, but they had been three life changing months for Alice. Travelling around Asia with Jules had changed her perspective on things in ways she couldn't have imagined back in her schooldays.

The two of them went through immigration which seemed endless, there was so many arriving passengers to process. Would he be there on the other side? Would he wait that long? They had spoken briefly a couple of times by phone and he had promised to meet her at the airport.

"I can't believe how nervous you are," Jules said. Her hair was braided into hundreds of tiny plaits and like Alice she was tanned from all the lazing around on beaches. "He's crazy about you. It won't have worn off in three months."

They finally made it through to baggage reclaim and customs. As they hauled their bags off the conveyor belt Alice felt self conscious about how much like backpackers they looked.

Jules slipped off as soon as they were through to find a bathroom. Alice knew that she was trying to tactfully disappear. She walked by herself through the gauntlet of other passengers' friends and relatives, numerous hotel chauffeurs waving placards, tour guides trying to assemble parties, feeling horribly alone for a moment.

And there he was.

He was more bronzed and even better looking than she remembered. And taller, and more serious. She felt a sudden panic. But then he saw her and his face lit up.

He came over and they stood for a moment in front of one another, and then his arms were around her and she was pressed against his chest and it felt like coming home.

She had missed him so much. From the way he was holding her she knew he felt the same.

When he finally let go they were both still awkward around one another. "How was the flight?" he asked.

"Not too bad. We were near the back."

"Your timing's perfect anyway." By a miracle he was actually in Brisbane the day they arrived, though he would have flown up from Sydney otherwise.

Alice suddenly remembered. "I forgot to ask! How was play?"

He grinned. "Not too bad." After returning to Australia he'd been a surprise re-selection for the national cricket team. Australia was currently playing a test series against the West Indies.

Stewart insisted on carrying her backpack as they walked towards the taxi rank. "Hadn't we better find Jules first?" he asked.

"She'll meet us outside. She's got the details of some backpacker hostel in Brisbane where we can stay."

Stewart stopped and turned her towards him. "Alice, you're not staying in a backpacker hostel. I've got you both a room in the hotel we're at. I could only get one because they were booked out, if you two don't mind sharing."

A hotel would be like paradise after some of the places they had stayed at in South East Asia. Even Mush's van would have been luxury in comparison. Clean towels. A working shower. Hopefully no cockroaches.

"God no, we won't mind sharing. We've been sharing dorms with loads of other people for the past few months," she told him.

"Of course you can stay with me in my room instead if you want."

She saw the faint doubt in his eyes. He was actually worried she would prefer to stay with Jules, that she might not want to share his room.

"What do you think?" she asked.

"That if you want to just sleep the whole night that's fine, but I'd really like to be with you."

She answered him with a kiss. He hadn't kissed her yet, and what was intended to be a brief embrace quickly deepened. His body felt harder than ever under his shirt - all the training probably - and she knew that she would have no desire to go straight to sleep that night.

I'm back, Alice thought. I'm where I should be. I'm where I want to always be.

The spell was broken when she heard the world's least authentic coughing behind her. Jules had found them.

"Great news," Alice said before Jules could make any embarrassing comments about fond reunions. "We're in a hotel tonight."

"Really?"

"The whole weekend if you want," Stewart said. "Until we fly back, which isn't until Wednesday."

As they got into the taxi Jules asked him how the match was going.

"Good, though it will be a miracle if I last the series," he said. "My shoulder flared up again."

"Is it painful when you play?"

"Not after a cortisone injection." He had planned to retire the previous year anyway, so a final international season was a huge bonus.

The light was fading as they drove into the centre of Brisbane and to the hotel. They got Jules checked in and went off to their respective rooms.

The hotel room was indeed like heaven compared to the last hostel they had been in. An expanse of clean white sheets, pillows, towels, it was just immaculate. Alice was reminded of the first time she had stayed at his place and suddenly felt shy.

"I know exactly what I'd like to do right now, but I came straight from the game so I'll shower first," he said.

Alice wouldn't have minded but hours on a plane and in the stickiness of Denpasar and Brisbane airports made her long for hot, clean water as well. She looked at him, a question in her eyes.

Within minutes she was in the hot steam with him, naked, both of them rediscovering one another. He was more taut and muscled than before but as tender as he was passionate.

Afterwards they lay on the bed together, the pristine sheets in crumpled disarray.

"Do you... still..." she felt insecure because he hadn't said it.

"Do I still love you? I love you more than ever. I've missed you more than I ever thought possible."

"I love you too. I was worried you wouldn't feel the same," she said.

"Three months isn't that long, not for me anyway. It felt like forever, waiting for you. I know you need to go on travelling with Jules but I want you here with me for a while first."

He only had to say something like this to her and she was ready for him all over again. He was in such supreme fitness that even after a long day on the cricket pitch he could meet her every need.

The next day they went to watch the test match at the Gabba, the Brisbane Cricket Ground. He had got them access to a special area by the player's enclosure which made them feel smug as there were other backpackers slumming it on the Hill.

Watching Stewart on the pitch transformed the play for Alice. He was opening the batting and she was on the edge of her seat throughout. Every time he cracked some runs it was ecstasy. Every time he faced a close call it was an absolute ordeal.

Jules was laughing at her. "You need a drink. Even Becky wasn't this bad watching Brett."

As the score climbed the tension only got even higher. It was such a hot, humid day in the subtropical Queensland heat. Alice wondered how the players weren't suffering heat exhaustion, standing out there hour after hour with no shade.

But they battled on and suddenly the scoreboard flicked over to three digits by his name and the crowd was in uproar at the century.

Even Jules was on her feet, dancing around, hugging Alice. "He got a tonne! I can't believe he got a tonne, he was supposed to be retired!"

Alice felt the happiest she had ever been in the world. It was her man that everyone was cheering. Celebrating. She had never experienced anything like this before and it felt amazing.

The match ended up drawn but she didn't care. Nothing could take away from Stewart's achievement. He was Man of the Match and there were people all over him. Press, fans, officials. Alice enjoyed the thrill of being the one who was with him though he was keeping their connection discreet for her sake, now he was in the spotlight again.

Not that they were doing anything wrong but she didn't want to end up in the tabloids here or back home. The secrecy made it feel a bit like being back at school, except the worst that could happen if they were exposed here was a few cameras in her face. Better that than Mr Francis and his lectures.

Later at the hotel, when it was finally just the two of them again, he made love to her with surprising stamina.

"Aren't you exhausted from today?" she asked him, as he took her body over the edge yet again.

"It was the thought of you up there watching me that did it," he told her. "I couldn't screw it up with you there."

They were both glistening with sweat despite the air-conditioning.

"I really made a difference?" She was sure he wasn't serious but she loved that he implied it.

"I want you at all the matches, if it doesn't mess up your travel plans. I'll fly you out and back. Then when we're done you can come and stay with me in Sydney for as long as you want."

Alice was so shattered from the hours in the heat, the excitement of the game and his lovemaking that she thought she would sleep forever. But she found herself waking in the night, or the early hours of the morning.

He was already awake, and he moved over her, gently sliding inside her again. She was always ready for him. Insatiable for him.

"If you still want me by next August, I'll come back to England with you," he said.

"Really? What about cricket?"

"Regardless of how this series goes I won't survive another one. The shoulder won't stand it, and I'm happy to go out on a high."

Alice ran a hand over his shoulder, feeling over the muscles that caused him so much trouble. On the surface it seemed perfect, his skin bronzed by the Australian sun. "I would so love you to be there."

They discussed the future while they lay together. Getting a job wouldn't be a problem for him, though it would likely be in London or one of the counties. It depended whether he took a coaching job or a role in sports management. With the current series going so well for him there would be many doors open.

"Even if I'm not in the same city as your university, it's not like England's a big place," he said.

Alice was starting to realise that. Compared with Australia anyway, where there was no choice but to fly if you wanted to get to another major city within a day. Back home you could drive anywhere in the country in a couple of hours or so.

"Whatever happens, every day I spend with you is worth it," he told her.

"And you're still ok with waiting?" She continued to worry she was holding him back.

"We have all the time in the world. I'd never rush you. Besides, I'll have a whole new career to start as well." He idly caressed her breasts and her stomach, making her shiver.

Then he looked into her eyes. "I didn't know I could feel like this. You've changed everything for me."

He had never spoken to her before quite like this. He had said words that were similar, but now his tone was more serious, more intense. It was the first time he had seemed vulnerable and it moved her. He was older than her, he had so much more life experience than her, yet she had the capacity to affect him in this way.

But she didn't feel scared. If he had said this to her six months ago she might have panicked.

Now, she felt completely as he did. The love she felt for him was constant, it had grown during the time they had spent together and the time apart. She wanted a future with him.

Outside the sun was rising. They had left the blinds half open and it was beautiful. It was the start of another summer, they had escaped winter altogether. Alice had first fallen in love with Stewart half a year ago, at the start of the English summer. Now she was on the edge of a second summer and a new, deeper phase of their love.

Epilogue II

Beloved, thou hast brought me many flowers
Plucked in the garden, all the summer through

Sonnets from the Portuguese XLIV
Elizabeth Barrett Browning

To South Africa, November 2002

Ten years ago Alice had escaped the grey grizzle of England for the Southern Hemisphere sun. Although they'd travelled backwards and forwards between Australia and the UK many times over the past decade, this felt like a milestone. She wondered if Stewart realised the anniversary as well.

"It's ten years this month, isn't it? Nearly to the day when you first landed in Brisbane."

Like so often during their time together he had read her mind.

"We're doing the right thing aren't we? You are happy about the move?" She was excited herself, but still anxious whether it was the right choice for all of them.

"It's only for ten months. And the kids will love it."

Alice looked down at the tousled blond heads of their sleeping twins. Thankfully they were both amazing travellers for such young toddlers. They'd had to be, with relatives on opposite sides of the world.

The four of them were flying to visit Alice's old boss Jo and her husband Pieter. One of the vets at the sanctuary Jo ran was going on maternity leave and Alice would be filling in for her. It was a dream opportunity. She'd initially been hesitant to accept but then Stewart had landed an amazing role with the South African cricket team, which would have been even crazier to turn down.

Sometimes Alice still marvelled at how perfect her life was. Since falling in love with Stewart she had never wanted anyone else, her feelings for him had only grown. Her desire too. Even after having the twins he could make her insides melt merely by looking at her in a certain way.

Chloe stirred and Alice stroked her head to settle her. The longer they slept the better. The little girl had insisted on wearing her tiger costume to the airport, even though they had tried to explain to her that there were no tigers in Africa.

Caspian, who was so much the spitting image of his father that Alice sometimes wondered if she had cloned him, was by far the quieter one of the pair.

"I was so nervous flying to Brisbane that time. Remember Jules with her hair all braided? We looked like such a couple of backpackers."

Stewart laughed. "Not a style she's managed to repeat." Jules had realised her dream of becoming a corporate lawyer and worked in aviation. She spent half her life travelling, usually in first class, and had racked up more air miles than she could ever use.

Becky and Brett had done well too. He'd enjoyed several years playing for Australia and now worked in sports marketing. Becky had specialised in sports physiotherapy which had made it easier for her to travel with him. They had two children as well, older than the twins.

"It's been summer almost always since I met you," Alice said. "We always seem to escape winter."

"It's because you look so sensational in a bikini," he told her.

She loved that he still thought this about her. He had also kept his athletic figure and barely looked a day older from when she had first met him.

Alice had a strange, fleeting memory of the fear she had felt all those years ago, when she had been summoned to explain her "inappropriate relationship" with him. Stewart saw the faint shadow pass across her face.

"Something wrong?"

"No, I was just having a strange flashback to Fairmount," she told him. "Wondering what Mr Francis and Mrs Paddington would think about us now."

"Are they both still there?"

"I think she is, though she must be due to retire soon. He moved to run a school in the north of England a year or so after we all left," Alice said. The school spirit had been jubilant at the departure of the Padlock by all accounts.

Thinking about Cheltenham reminded Alice of her parents. She had been feeling quite sad about missing another Christmas with them that year. They had spent the previous year with Stewart's family in Sydney and they usually tried to alternate.

"In case you still have cold feet about the move," he said, reading the slight shadow that was passing across her face, "I have a surprise for you."

"What?"

"Since it's our tenth Christmas together I thought it should be a big one. So everyone's coming, your mother, Richard, your brothers. And all my lot too," he told her.

Alice was overjoyed. "Really? How did you arrange all that?"

"It wasn't difficult. Your family were only too happy for some winter sun, and mine can't bear to miss a single Christmas with the twins."

It was the best news ever. It made the trip completely perfect. Her brothers were both at Fairmount now, excelling at maths and science like Richard had. They were wonderful uncles to the twins despite still being schoolboys themselves.

"And your sister?" Alice had become firm friends with her sister-in-law even though she didn't get to see her very often.

"Yes, with her brood as well."

Alice sat back and wondered about the journey they were taking. "It will probably fly by, won't it? And be over before we know it."

"We can always bring back a souvenir. A cub maybe."

"I don't think they let you take lion cubs out of the country. I'm sure the twins will be begging to though," she said.

"That wasn't the kind of cub I had in mind." His eyes flicked briefly to her stomach and back to her eyes.

She felt her stomach flip at his gaze. Just the fact that he wanted to get her pregnant again made her weak with lust for him. They had only planned on having two children and the twins had been a happy surprise to arrive as soon as they did. She had no idea he was keen on more.

"You could handle all that again?" He'd been amazing the first time around, all the sleepless nights and helping with feeding. Double the trouble as well, being twins.

"The thought of you carrying my child again is enough to make me try for it here and now," he told her.

"I don't think the pilot would be very pleased."

He grinned at her and she blushed, knowing he was thinking of a flight to Sydney they'd taken a few years ago when they'd been upgraded to Club Class. It had led to them joining a rather more exclusive, if illicit, club as well.

With two infants to mind that kind of behaviour was on hold for now, but she knew he wouldn't be letting her get much sleep after they landed, given the desire in his eyes now.

It would be dusk below but above the clouds the sunset was still burning up the sky in an apricot-gold fire. Its light streamed through the window onto them all. Stewart always looked golden to her; now he was literally gilded.

"I love you," he said to her.

"I love you too."

He was all she would ever want. There could never be anyone else. He was her love, her joy, her desire and she was his. An eternal summer, that would never fade.

Author's Note

While all the characters in this book are fictitious, the events portrayed are as historically accurate as possible. The free party or rave scene in the UK was in full swing in the late 1980s and 1990s. The raves described in *Summer's Edge* took place on the dates and locations mentioned, culminating in the great Castlemorton Common Festival towards the end of May 1992 which attracted up to 40,000 people.

The arrests of some of those involved in the festival eventually resulted in much of the free party movement moving over to Europe.

Concerns about Castlemorton also led to legislation in the Criminal Justice and Public Order Act 1994, which outlawed outdoor parties playing *"sounds wholly or predominantly characterised by the emission of a succession of repetitive beats."*

All the county cricket matches as well as the Australian Test match also took place on the dates and locations between the teams mentioned. The players, the order of play, and any results given are entirely fictitious.

About Noël Cades

Noël Cades is a British writer who currently lives in Sydney, Australia. A fan of romance from historic to erotic, some of Noël's favourite authors include Jilly Cooper, Jackie Collins, Elizabeth Rolls and Victoria Holt.

Noël is always delighted to hear from other fans, readers and writers of romance.

You can contact Noël at noelcades@gmail.com

Noël's blog is at http://noelcades.tumblr.com

Visit Noël's blog to sign up for exclusive news and the chance to receive new free book giveaways.